The Dante Inferno:

Dante's Dilemma: Romero

The Dante Dynasty Series:
Book #10

by

Day Leclaire

USA Today Bestselling Author

Please Note

For more information, please visit my website: http://www.DayLeclaire.com

Book Description

Romero Dante: The town bad boy. The man all good girls should avoid.

Julietta Bianchi: Sweet and virginal. The woman who'd do anything to save her family. And engaged to Rom's best friend.

Rom Dante had always been warned about the danger of The Inferno. After all, it creates an all-consuming, love-at-first-touch lust, which led to his mother's ruin ... and Rom's birth. Now it strikes again with the one woman Rom can't have—Julietta Bianchi, the fiancée of his best friend.

Julietta will do whatever necessary to save her family from financial disaster, even marry a man she doesn't love. But days before her wedding is to take place, her heart is stolen—with a single touch. Now the two lovers must choose between honor ... and each other.

But Romero's grandfather warns that to ignore The Inferno will turn love from a blessing to a curse. And Rom can't allow that, even if it means stealing his bride and forcing her to the altar.

Dedication

To Mom

Hazen Haile Fairbank Totton

With love and gratitude.

Your memory lives on in your children,
grandchildren, and great-grandchildren,
including your special namesake.

Table of Contents

Other Titles by Day Leclaire

The Dante Inferno:
The Dante Dynasty Series

*Some blazes, once ignited, can't be extinguished. Just one burning touch connects a Dante with his soul mate.
The Inferno ... curse or blessing?*

Chapter One

The village of Santa Lucia, Tuscany, Italy

Early June 1956

Spring sweetened the air of the Tuscan countryside, and Romero Dante breathed it in as though it were some rare nectar. And perhaps it was. He'd spent so many years in Florence, both attending University and apprenticing with his Dante relatives in order to learn the craft of jewelry design and creation, he'd forgotten how amazing home smelled. How would his friends and family react to the man he'd become? Would they welcome him? Or would they still consider him the town bastard, the bad boy of Santa Lucia? Not that it mattered. He wouldn't be staying long.

He shrugged off his suit jacket and slung it over one shoulder before rolling up the sleeves of his crisp, white shirt to expose the light smattering of dark hairs across sun-kissed forearms. A battered truck, its flatbed piled high with vegetables, slowly approached from the direction of the small village of Santa Lucia, heading in the opposite direction. Rom lifted an arm in greeting. Dust containing the rich, alluvial soil that fed the nearby grapevines rose behind in a magnificent rooster tail. Picked up by a light breeze, it coated the wild garlic growing along the roadside.

The driver honked and rattled to a slow stop, the metal railings surrounding the flatbed clanging in protest. "Is that you, Romero?"

Rom waved aside a lingering cloud of dust and grinned. "Alive and in the flesh, Aldo. How's it going?"

"Can't complain. I see you're just in time for Tito Rossi's engagement party. Have you met his bride-to-be?"

"I will tomorrow night at the party. Why?"

Aldo's dark eyes sparkled with mischief. "You should see the girl he's had to settle for. No one else would have him, of course. Not when *il Rossi* is as stupid as he is poor."

It was a running joke since Tito was the eldest son of the richest man in their small town and a success at any business endeavor he attempted. "How ugly is she?"

"She is as round as she is tall, with a face every bit as lovely as my prize sow."

Rom lifted an eyebrow. "Then why is Tito marrying her?"

"Your good friend has decided to become a vintner and compete with your stepfather and his sons. The family of his precious bride-to-be owns land he wants for his vineyard."

"They're refusing to sell it to him?"

Aldo nodded. "They claim it must remain in the family. If Tito becomes family, they are happy to sell the land." He grinned, a slash of white teeth against his dark olive complexion. "For a hefty price, of course."

"Of course."

"Eh, you know how it is," Aldo said. "Tito Rossi is rich. His bride has a dozen sisters—"

"Truly? A dozen?"

Aldo shrugged. "Maybe only six or eight. *Non me ne frega niente*. What does it matter? It is a business arrangement, even if Tito appears smitten with the girl."

Rom patted his trouser pocket, relieved to feel the small bulge made by the box containing Tito's engagement ring, a ring his friend had commissioned him to design. He'd be in deep trouble if he lost it. "I'm relieved to hear Tito has serious feelings for her."

Serious feelings or not, Rom hoped the ring he'd designed, and named, *"L'amore Vero"*—or True Love—wasn't meant to forever join a couple in a marriage of convenience. His ring possessed a heart and soul, as did all the pieces he created. It was meant to celebrate the sort of love that lasted a lifetime.

Aldo gave a short, cynical laugh. "Has a woman existed who Tito hasn't fallen in love with? My sister hasn't stopped crying since the banns were read. Your friend broke her heart, though I tell you privately, I think it is a good thing. He would not have remained faithful to her."

"If I had any sisters, I'd lock them away whenever he showed his pretty face," Rom conceded. "But Tito doesn't do it on purpose. He simply loves women."

"Not my sister, he doesn't. Not if I have anything to say about it." Aldo ground the gears of his truck. "Now he will marry his vineyards, my sister will wed Vincenzo, and that will be the end of it, *lodare Dio*."

Rom nodded. "Praise God, indeed. Vincenzo is a good man. He works hard for a living and is honorable and even-tempered. You couldn't ask for better."

"Best of all, he puts up with Caterina's nonsense. For that alone, I thank him. *Vado,* Rom. I have a delivery to make and am already late."

"*Ciao,* Aldo. I will see you tomorrow night, no?"

"*Ma, che sei grullo?* Of course, you'll see me there. Wine will flow. Food will burden the tables. There will be a full moon. So, we will laugh and sing and steal kisses from many women. I wouldn't miss it." He released the clutch and continued down the road, his arm lifted in farewell.

Rom noticed some wild sorrel growing beside a limestone wall bordering the road and tugged free several stalks. It would be a perfect gift to offer his *nonno*. His grandfather possessed a vegetable and herb garden that sparked the envy of the entire village, as well as an unrivaled talent in the kitchen, a gift he'd passed on to Rom. The sorrel would be a welcome addition for *Nonno's* chickpea soup or perhaps to add to the sauce for tomorrow's eggs. Rom vaulted the limestone wall bordering the road to take advantage of a shortcut across an uncultivated field filled with wildflowers and blossoming orange trees.

And that's when he saw her.

From one heartbeat to the next, The Inferno, the bane of his family, forever changed his life. Time skittered to a stop, stilling all sound and slowing all movement. In that moment Rom knew the image before him would remain part of the fiber of his being for the rest of his life, indelibly branded into the weft and warp of who he was . . . and who he'd eventually become. He sensed the change, like a page turning on the book chronicling his life, opening to a new chapter with an unexpected twist in what was to come.

She knelt in the shade of one of the trees, surrounded by wildflowers—royal purple hyacinth, chaste white daisies, and a smattering of bright red poppies, her innocent bloom of youth just ripening into the heady flush of adulthood. A straw hat rested in the grass beside her, trailing soft pink ribbons, while a large basket squatted at her elbow, half filled with a selection of blossoms. She wore a simple cotton dress, the afternoon sun shooting soft rays of gold through the thin material, outlining her full, round breasts and the tiniest waist he'd ever seen.

She is yours, whispered the sun.

She hummed while she worked, her hands moving gracefully among the flowers, snipping the choicest ones. A gentle breeze kicked up and stirred the orange blossoms overhead, sending them raining down on to her hair. They landed like dainty white stars captured in an endless current of hip-length ringlets containing every shade of brown imaginable.

She is meant for you, sighed the wind.

His heart and soul concurred. He wanted her as he'd wanted nothing before in his life. He didn't know who she was, didn't really care. He simply understood on some primal level that she belonged to him, just as he belonged to her.

Take her! Take the woman. The earthy words echoed through him, filling him, overwhelming him with a desire so strong, he shook with it. He didn't dare approach her, not until he regained his self-control. He lowered his head, fighting for focus. For clarity.

He knew what this was. How could he not when his mother, Nicci, had warned him from the time he'd been a baby? Warned him about the Dante curse that ran through her side of the family. It was the dreaded Inferno, a disease of the blood, passed from one generation to the next. A craving that overcame all inhibition and stole intellect and reason, leading those who suffered from it to their ruin. It was an inescapable desire that drove sense and sensibility from the mind, leaving behind a lust so strong he didn't have a hope of evading it.

After all, The Inferno was responsible for his conception and birth. As well as his mother's shame. His mother had experienced the curse and had indulged in an ill-fated affair. Then her lover had died, leaving her pregnant and disgraced.

The fact that Rom's stepfather had overlooked her indiscretion and had even given her bastard child a home—if not his name—was considered a marvel by everyone in Santa Lucia. Since then, Nicci had led a pious life, keeping a spotless home, devoting herself to the care and feeding of her family, all the while attending daily Mass. But she'd warned Rom of the dangers. Warned Rom that the Dantes were cursed.

Not that it changed a damn thing. The words came again, echoing from head to heart, seeping into his very bones.

Get. The. Woman.

The young woman clipped another blossom and lifted it to her face, the red of the poppy the same shade as her sun-kissed cheeks and ripe, full lips. A molten ribbon of passion burned through Rom and seemed to stretch toward her, connecting them. And all the while, he heard the desperate demand urging him to cross the field to her side. To take her into his arms and strip away the clothes separating them, and make her his. Make her his right here, with wildflowers for their bed, orange blossoms for their canopy, and the scent of love perfuming the air.

He must have made some sort of sound of desperation, for her head jerked in his direction, and her eyes widened in alarm, like a lamb spying its first wolf. She reached for her basket of flowers, clutching it close, as though for protection. He paused, waging an impossible battle between caution and desire.

"I didn't mean to startle you," he finally said, the words low and hard-won. "I was cutting through the field on my way home."

She glanced uneasily in the direction of Santa Lucia. "You live near here?"

"Another couple of miles. I'm Rom Dante."

"Julietta Bianchi. My family and I live a few hours further west. We're visiting."

He grinned at that, amazed he could find anything the least humorous about his situation. "Romero and Julietta? What are the odds?"

That had her laughing, a sweet, pure sound that called to him. He answered the call, slowly approaching. He could see her eyes now. They were a lovely hazel, an intriguing mix of green and gold and brown, the expression wavering between caution and something else. Attraction?

He could still hear the whispering voice of sin hammering at him, filling him with an unsettling awareness he could do nothing to suppress. Slowly, her amusement faded, replaced by a matching awareness. She stood, the basket of flowers tumbling to her feet, the contents surrounding her in a colorful pool of innocence and passion. The wild sorrel for Rom's grandfather slipped from his grasp, forgotten before it reached the ground.

He simply held out his hand, waiting to see if she took it. Eve tempted by the apple. Slowly, oh, so slowly, she slipped her hand into his. Eve biting the apple.

And that's when The Inferno took fire.

Rom felt Julietta's start of surprise, her expression reflecting shock at the burn passing from his palm to hers. It didn't actually hurt, certainly no more than a spark of static electricity. But the warmth lingered, sinking through flesh into bone, strengthening and quickening with each beat of their hearts, bonding them physically, as well as on some deeper, more spiritual level. Where before desire wove them together, now that same desire sealed the bond, joining them through their linked hands.

This was a curse? Curses should be taken seriously. His mother had taught him so. Rom shook his head. No. The Inferno didn't seem evil. Not even a little. How could something so incredible be considered wicked? It wasn't possible. Instead, this felt ... He hesitated, a strange certainty filled him.

The Inferno felt like a gift. A blessing.

And as that certainty took hold, he gazed down at Julietta, his Inferno mate. "You're mine now," he stated.

Julietta stared at Rom in disbelief. Belatedly, she snatched her hand free from his. Not that it helped. The lingering effects of the electric shock when they'd first touched remained. She scrubbed her palm across her hip in an attempt to erase the sensation. That didn't help, either.

Nor did it stop the insistent tug of attraction. It washed over her, a determined tide bent on claiming all that stood in its way, forcing her relentlessly in a direction she'd never anticipated taking. While it stung, it also thrilled, awakening parts of her that had slept until this moment. No one's touch had ever affected her this way. Not even the one man whose touch should have stirred her to passion.

"What did you just do to me?" she demanded. "What was that?"

He folded his arms across his chest. "My family calls it The Inferno."

"The Inferno? Dante's *Inferno?* Oh, very amusing."

She glared at her palm, relieved to see The Inferno, or whatever Rom had done to her, hadn't left a visible mark. She'd never have been able to explain it to her family, let alone her fiancé. Of course, that didn't erase the other mark—a mark invisible to the eye but which had somehow seared her heart and emotions in ways she'd never experienced before.

"We don't consider The Inferno a joke." A shadow edged his expression as though his thoughts had turned dark. "The Dantes take it very seriously," he added in a low, pained voice.

She glanced across the field, hoping to catch a glimpse of her mother and sisters. Why hadn't she stayed with them? Why had she gone off on her own? She cast Rom an uneasy look. He was a tall man, well over six feet, broad and strong through the shoulders and chest. He wore a suit with casual elegance, his jacket slung over one shoulder. His features were too defined to be considered handsome in the conventional sense, and yet they were patrician, etched with a nobility that drew her. His hair was a deep ebony, contrasting with the most unusual eyes she'd ever seen, a brilliant antique gold that gave him an air of wisdom beyond his years. They mesmerized her, holding her with a power she couldn't ignore. And when she looked—*really* looked—she relaxed infinitesimally.

These weren't the eyes of a crazed person or someone who wished her harm. They reflected the character of a man who possessed fierce honor and intelligence, strength tempered with compassion. They drew her in, claimed her.

Owned her.

She took a swift step backward, crushing several of her precious blossoms underfoot. With an exclamation of alarm, she knelt and began to gather them, returning them to her basket. Rom crouched beside her.

"Here, let me help."

"There's no need. I can do it."

He ignored her, patiently picking up each fragile stalk and adding it to the basket. "It won't go away, you know."

"What won't?" Foolish question when her palm continued to tingle and itch, and desire ate at her like a hunger she couldn't satisfy. Didn't dare satisfy. She forced herself to look at him, indirectly acknowledging the reality of The Inferno by reframing her question. "How do you know it won't go away?"

"I just know."

She heard the truth in his words and rocked back on to her heels. "Have you felt it before? Is that how you know it's this Inferno?"

He looked up from his self-appointed task, and she suppressed a shiver of need at the heat reflected in his golden eyes. "I've never experienced The Inferno before, and something tells me I never will again. I wouldn't want to, not with anyone other than you." He hesitated as though weighing some private set of facts. "I think The Inferno allows Dantes to find their soul mates. How else can you explain what just happened between us?"

"You are crazy, Romero Dante," she informed him fiercely. Or maybe she spoke with such vehemence in an attempt to convince herself. "I am *not* your soul mate. I can't be. I won't be."

"Words don't change facts. We are meant for each other." He tilted his head to one side and grinned, causing a shaft of desire to rip through her. "Deny it all you want, but I can see that you want me, even though we've only known each other a few minutes."

Madre di Dio, what was he doing to her? His words wove a spell around and through her, the scent of orange blossoms and hyacinth combining to seal the charm. From this day forward she'd always associate their perfume with this moment in time, with Rom and his wicked Inferno and her sinful, ungovernable passion.

She'd always had "the sight," and today proved no different. She could see herself on a pathway, one that diverged a few paces ahead. The right-hand fork led in the direction mapped out by her family. It was a comfortable, well-worn path, one that women in her family had taken for endless generations before her. Leafy orange trees lined the way, their fading blossoms carpeting the ground like snow. At the end of the path stood a smiling man who would provide her with a comfortable life and healthy children.

To the left a second path beckoned, full of twists and turns that made it difficult to see clearly. Trees also lined this path, though none were orange trees. Instead they were apples and cherries, peaches and olives, all heavy with fruit. And in the middle of the pathway stood Rom, burning with a light so bright it hurt to look at him. Did she turn left toward the unknown, or right along the road she'd been told to take? How could she continue down the easier path when every fiber of her being urged her to turn aside and take a different road? One that led to Rom.

"The attraction will fade." Did he hear the desperation underscoring her words?

"It will never fade, not even if we live another hundred years."

She snatched up a final few poppies and dropped them into the basket at her feet. "You try this Inferno nonsense on all the girls around here, don't you? You tell them you're their soul mate and then seduce them. Poor, foolish women, falling for your fairy tales. Well, it's not going to work with me."

He simply laughed. "Shall I prove you wrong?"

"There's nothing you can say or do that will change my mind. Now, if you'll excuse me—"

He cupped her chin in his large hand and leaned in, his mouth hovering above hers for a split second. And then he kissed her. It was as though he reached into her heart and touched her soul. That simple joining of lips sparked a wildfire unlike anything she'd ever known. She'd been kissed before, but never like this. Nor had those kisses stirred the blaze of need that flooded through every part of her.

She heard a soft moan, vaguely aware it came from her. He responded by drawing her closer, into a tight embrace, his arms hard and firm around her back. And she let him. She did more than let him. She slid her hands up his chest and around his neck, her fingers arrowing into the crisp, dark waves of his hair to anchor him against her.

His kiss deepened, and she felt his tongue tease her lips. She'd heard that men liked to kiss with their mouths open, touching tongues. But she'd never tried it before. She'd never even been tempted. Until now.

With a soft sigh, she opened her mouth to him, reveling in the delicious sensation of his tongue against hers. She dueled with him, a teasing thrust and parry she suspected mimicked true lovemaking. She barely noticed when he tipped her backward into the embrace of the warm, fragrant grass, or the way his broad shoulders shielded her from the piercing rays of the late afternoon sun.

Her hair formed a soft pillow around her head, the ringlets trembling in agitation against her temples, echoing the tumble of emotions racing through her. She welcomed Rom's weight, heavy against her breasts and hips, delighting in the way their legs tangled, mirroring their lips and tongues. And she pulled him closer still.

Rom cupped her breast, his thumb circling the tip, causing her nipple to harden. It wasn't enough. Not nearly enough. He must have felt the same way because he unbuttoned the bodice of her cotton dress and swept it from her shoulders. She wore only a thin slip beneath, transparent enough that he could see the duskiness of her nipples through the fabric.

"Bellezza," he murmured against her skin. "You are the most beautiful woman I have ever seen."

"This is wrong. We need to stop."

"And we will." A shadow moved across his expression again, tarnishing the brilliance of his eyes. "I will do nothing to dishonor you, I promise."

"You don't understand. I've dishonored myself. I'm en—"

Rom took her nipple between his teeth and tugged. The words vanished, unspoken. Thought vanished. All that remained was pure sensation. The breath caught in her lungs, and all she could do was hold on . . . and let go. Her head tipped back, and she stared up at the orange tree and the canopy of blossoms raining gently on to them.

It was the orange blossoms that finally brought her to her senses. "Please, stop," she whispered.

He heard her, even as softly as she'd spoken. He lifted off of her, carefully adjusting her slip and sliding the bodice of her dress closed. She attempted to button it, but her fingers were trembling so badly she couldn't manage. So Rom completed the task for her.

"I can't come to you tonight," he said. "I have other obligations."

"So do I," she said. She prayed her legs would hold her as she stood. The flowers had spilled out of her basket again. Not that it mattered anymore. They'd been crushed beneath her, ruined in a painfully symbolic way. "I can't see you again, Rom."

"I've already explained to you. The Inferno—"

"The Inferno doesn't matter."

"Of course it matters. We are joined now. We will marry. I will meet your family and declare my intentions. After a reasonable span of time, we'll have the banns read."

"Stop. Stop it, Rom." She forced herself to meet his gaze. "We aren't joined. We won't marry. And you'll never speak of what happened here. You can't. It would bring dishonor to us both."

He stilled. "Why is that, Julietta?"

"Because I'm engaged to be married. My engagement party is tomorrow night."

He stared in shocked disbelief. "Tito? You're Tito's bride?"

She nodded, shame filling her. "And in another week, I'll be his wife."

With that, she turned and ran. Ran from the one man she wanted more than all others. The one man she couldn't have.

Chapter Two

Julietta worked alongside her mother, Maria, and older sister, Serena, putting the final touches on the delicacies they planned to serve at tomorrow's engagement celebration.

Since their own village was so far away, the Rossi family had kindly provided them with a lovely stone cottage in which to stay for the duration of the wedding preparations, not far from the huge villa that housed Tito's family. The cottage was the original home for the Rossis before the villa had been built. Heavily damaged during the war, the ancient structure had been repaired and renovated. Even so, some of the original house remained, the rough stones imbued with the passage of endless generations.

So many Rossis. They smothered her with their ghostly presence, especially after what had happened in the meadow with Rom Dante. Julietta kept her head down and focused on the job at hand, praying no one looked too closely at her. If they did, they'd see what she'd done, for surely the guilt of it must be emblazoned on her face and glittering in her eyes.

Sure enough, her mother paused in her labors. "What's wrong, Julietta?" she asked.

But it was Serena who responded. "She's nervous about tomorrow night."

Her mother frowned. "What is there to be nervous about? It's a party, for goodness' sake."

"I don't love Tito." The words escaped in a rush. "And he doesn't love me."

Maria gave a quick laugh. "Well, of course you don't. That will come in time. Do you think your *babbo* loved me when we were first married?" She gave a dainty snort. "Not at all. And look at us now, eight daughters later with the first of you about to wed."

"I'd always hoped" —*dreamed*— "that I could go to University and get a job in Florence." While her father had encouraged her dream, her mother had always claimed she was too progressive for her own good. Apparently, that sort of progressiveness would end badly for her, though precisely how had never been explained.

"And where would the money come from?" Maria scolded. "You must be practical, Julietta. Did the war teach you nothing? Granted, you were only seven when it ended, but that is still old enough to remember how many lives it destroyed. How many family members it stole from us, including those of your uncles." She crossed herself. "Better to keep your head down and marry a man who can care for you. Protect you. See to your welfare. Tito can do all of those things."

"Tito should be marrying Serena. She's older than me."

"You know perfectly well I promised God if we came safely through the war, I would give your sister to the church. And though we suffered greatly, we did survive." She eyed her daughters sternly. "I am a woman who keeps her promises, just as Serena is a loving and dutiful daughter who fully appreciates her family obligations. That is why I insisted Tito choose you, Julietta."

"Rosa has the calling, Mamma, not me," Serena commented placidly. "If I were marrying Tito, I would make him a good wife."

"Wait." Julietta took a swift step backward. "You *insisted* Tito marry me?"

One look at her daughter had Maria altering her words. "Perhaps 'insisted' is too strong a word. I *encouraged* his choice." Defensiveness crept into her tone. "It didn't take much urging. You're a beautiful woman. He didn't care which of you he married, so long as you were a well-behaved girl."

Bitterness filled her. "You mean, so long as it meant he could buy our vineyards."

"That will be quite enough of that," her mother retorted sharply. "What's done is done, and we must be realistic if we're to have any sort of future. You and Tito marry next week. He will buy your father's vineyards. And we will never have to worry about money again. He is a respectable man who will be generous to his bride, especially if she keeps him happy."

"She means in bed," Serena supplied.

Maria rapped a wooden spoon against the countertop. *"Basta così!* How do you expect the church to take you when you can't keep a civil tongue in your mouth?"

Serena simply smiled. "That won't be a problem since I don't have a vocation to the life."

"Zitta," Maria said in a tone that warned she'd reached the end of her rope. "See what mischief your sisters are getting into. And don't think I won't have words with *il sacerdote* about this."

"I wish you would. Maybe he'll be able to convince you that I'll never make a proper nun. He's certainly told me often enough."

The instant Serena left the room, Julietta said, "I wish you would let Serena marry Tito. She actually wants him. Plus, I think she understands what it will take to be a good wife to him."

"Your sister is for the church," her mother insisted stubbornly. "As for the rest, you'll figure it out."

"He won't stay faithful to me."

Her mother stiffened. "And how do you know this?"

Julietta ducked her head. "Some of the women I've met in Santa Lucia have said things."

"Men are rarely faithful to their wives," Maria finally admitted. "What *is* important is that he cares for you, provides for you, and that you care for him, and provide him with children. Preferably male children. Maybe if I'd given your father sons instead of daughters, we wouldn't have to sell the vineyard."

"Mamma—"

Maria wiped her hands on her apron and turned to confront her daughter. "Would you dishonor your family, Julietta?" she demanded.

"No, of course not."

"Breaking off the engagement at this late date would bring dishonor to us all. The Rossi family would not take it well. I don't want to think what might happen if we were to get on their bad side. Please. I am begging you. Be an obedient daughter, Julietta Angelina. Marry Tito." She wrapped her arms around her daughter and gave her a swift hug. "He's not a bad man, is he?"

"No, Mamma," Julietta whispered.

"Has he hurt you in any way?"

She shook her head. "He's been very kind to me."

"Isn't that good enough?"

At one point she might have thought so. But not now. Not after what had happened in the field. The chaste kisses Tito had given her couldn't begin to compare to the heated exchanges with Rom Dante. With Tito, she'd felt nothing. Not passion, not distaste. Just . . . nothing. She attempted to imagine how she'd respond if Tito unbuttoned her dress. If he'd tugged aside her slip and caressed her breasts. If he'd kissed her nipples and teased them with his teeth.

And she shuddered in distaste.

No. She couldn't imagine doing with Tito what she'd done with Rom. It seemed wrong. Sacrilegious. Glancing down, she realized she'd dug her thumb into the palm of her hand in the exact spot where Rom had burned her with his "Inferno." It itched, a constant reminder of how she'd betrayed her fiancé. It wasn't Serena who needed to confess to *il sacerdote*. Her sins were far worse than her sister's.

What would happen when she confessed she didn't love Tito, didn't want him? What would happen when she confessed what she'd done with Rom? What she longed to do again?

"I'm going to hell," she whispered.

"What did you say?" Maria asked.

Julietta closed her eyes against the press of tears. "I'm not feeling well."

"We can't have you sick for your engagement party tomorrow. Go straight to bed. I'll send up a tray of chicken soup and fresh bread. I'm sure you'll feel better by morning."

Probably so. After all, she doubted she could feel any worse. And while she lay in bed, not sleeping, she'd concentrate on erasing all thought of Romero Dante.

If only she could also erase the escalating desire that wove like a ribbon of need through every part of her.

Rom's family celebrated his return with enthusiastic restraint. While they offered up hugs, kisses, and a table laden with food, it felt like the sort of greeting offered to a guest, not a son of the family. But then, he wasn't a true son, but a bastard. He didn't carry the Ranieri name, the name of his stepfather, Luigi, but his mother's. *Nonno* eased the burden of bearing the Dante name, since he was also one, and Rom had often wondered if his grandfather lived with them for that express purpose, to lend an air of legitimacy and acceptance to his grandson. His presence had certainly eased Rom's life and given him someone to talk to whenever life became difficult.

In addition to the food, bottles of wine bearing the Ranieri label cluttered the wooden table, as well as his *nonno's* homemade honey beer. Gossip about nearby friends and relatives flowed as freely as the drink, and he savored every moment of it with a bittersweet delight, aware that where once he'd belonged within the tightly woven fabric of Santa Lucia, on another level he had always stood outside its protective embrace and always would. Still, it was good to hear how the lives of the local villagers had changed or, more often, remained the same.

He dug his thumb into the palm of his right hand while he listened, not that it eased the itch created by The Inferno. If family legend ran true, he'd been changed by his connection to Julietta, just as he'd been changed from the youth he'd been five short years ago when he'd left home, a teenager intent on becoming a jewelry designer like his distant Dante relatives.

The years had branded him, much as The Inferno had, while home and hearth remained as it had always been. Living in *Firenze*— Florence—for the past several years had shaken most of the rustic from his boots. And though part of him remained rooted in the rich soil of his birthplace, another part had been forever altered during his apprenticeship and University studies in the city. He thought of the letter, tucked carefully in his trouser pocket. Soon it would undergo an even more drastic alteration.

Across from him, his mother gasped. "*Santa Maria, Madre di Dio!*"

At first, Rom didn't understand, not until he saw what had drawn his mother's attention. He glanced at his hands, at the way he dug his thumb into his palm. "Mamma—"

"It's the Dante curse. It's The Inferno." She burst into tears and crossed herself repeatedly. "Who? Who have you also cursed?"

"No, you don't understand. It's not a curse. It's a . . ."

The room had gone deathly silent, and his words trailed off. His stepfather glared at him in outrage, his expression mirrored by his three sons. As one, they stood. "Come, Nicci," Luigi said. He took her arm and helped her from her chair, drawing her close. He paused in the doorway to address Rom. "You will not shame your mother further, is it understood? If you do so, you will no longer be welcome here."

Rom had no idea how long he sat there, surrounded by the cooling remains of their dinner. He didn't wake to his surroundings until *Nonno* placed a hand on his shoulder. "Come with me, Romero."

His grandfather snagged a pair of beer bottles and inclined his head toward his garden. Rom followed, guilt waging a bitter war with defiance. They didn't understand. None of them. What he felt for Julietta wasn't a curse. He refused to believe it. Granted, a hint of desperation underscored his passion for her, but all men experienced that in the arms of a beautiful woman. And if his craving rose to a level he'd never known with any other, he refused to believe the connection between them resulted from a curse. Not when it felt so pure. So right.

So eternal.

A waxing moon, fast approaching full, cast a soft radiance over the fragrant garden. *Nonno* paused near his precious herbs, breaking off a bit of tarragon to roll between his gnarled fingers. Its lemony-licorice scent perfumed the night air. He sighed and eased himself on to a nearby bench.

"So. It has happened," he stated with devastating simplicity.

Rom didn't bother to deny it. "Yes."

"You do not seem overjoyed by this event. Is it because of what Luigi and your mother said?"

"No." He joined his grandfather, stretching his long legs across the flagstones paving the garden walkway and sipping his beer. "Okay, maybe a

little. They think it's a curse. But it's not It felt—
"

"More like a blessing?"

"Yes!" He straightened and turned to face his grandfather. "Yes. That is what I feel when I touch her. Like I've been blessed."

"And so you have." *Nonno* set aside his beer bottle and took Rom's hand in his, pressing his thumb into his grandson's palm. "Do you feel this itch? This burn that spreads deeper with each beat of your heart? That is not a curse. It is a message. You must listen to the message or suffer the consequences."

"What consequences?"

His grandfather's eyes—identical to Rom's own—pierced the darkness. "When you listen to The Inferno, when you do as it directs, your life will be blessed. This is why Dantes, other than your poor mamma, call it a blessing."

"Our Dante cousins say it's a blessing, too."

"Only they don't feel the burn, do they?"

Rom shook his head. "They all have marks on their palm they claim come from The Inferno."

Nonno inclined his head. "All Dantes are marked by The Inferno in some fashion. We feel the burn. They receive a mark. It does not matter, because the end result is the same. My cousins are smart. They heed the mark and are blessed. But if you ignore it, if you turn from The Inferno out of fear or ignorance or stubbornness, that blessing becomes a curse. For the rest of your life you will live with regret. If you marry another, one who is not your Inferno mate, that marriage will be a disaster for you both. Hear my warning, *nipote.*"

"That's not what happened with Mamma."

Nonno released a gusty sigh. "No, it is not," he agreed, a wealth of pain bleeding into his words. He hesitated, choosing his words with care. "Your mother was given the blessing at a very young age. Too young. The Inferno is an overpowering urge."

"She gave in to the urge." His jaw tightened. "Otherwise, I wouldn't be here."

Sadness deepened the lines of *Nonno's* face. "She did. And she was punished for it. The night you were conceived, she allowed lust to overcome what was right and proper, and her fiancé was taken from her. But no matter what anyone says, your father was a good man, Romero."

"She never speaks of him."

"No. To do so would dishonor her husband. Despite outward appearances, it has not been an easy existence for your mamma. Luigi continues to hold Nicci's disgrace over her head, watching for further weakness in case she brings shame to the Ranieri name. Since he rescued her from an unsavory life, she shows her gratitude by being a model wife and mother. Not that her piety makes him any less critical." *Nonno* shook his head in sorrow. "That is her curse for not playing by the rules The Inferno sets forth."

Rom took a moment to digest his grandfather's words, then asked the question he'd long wanted answered. "Am I like him? Am I like my father?"

Nonno sculpted Rom's face with gnarled fingers, as though committing his face to memory. "You have a Dante look about you. Even so, I see much of your father in various aspects. His intelligence. His determination. His interest in the world beyond his small village. He was a man capable of plucking the stars from the heavens if he so wished. I suspect he'd have gone far if he'd lived." *Nonno* rubbed his chest as though it ached. "Ah, it is so tragic, it hurts to think of it."

"He was hit by a car."

"Shortly after leaving your mamma's arms. Maybe if Nicci had not allowed The Inferno to get the better of her, he would never have died. Eh. *Chissà*." Pain trembled in his voice, making him sound far older than his years, old and defeated. "Who knows."

"Do you really believe that?"

A silent tear trickled down *Nonno's* cheek. "Only the good Lord can say, *nipote*. It is possible he would still have died." He drew a ragged breath. "I have thought about this for many years. And may God forgive me for my sinful thoughts. I would rather your mamma be disgraced, then never to have had you in my life."

Rom wrapped his grandfather in a fierce hug and thumped his fist against the old man's back. *"Ti amo, Nonno."*

"Ti amo, Romero." *Nonno* wiped away his tears and regarded his grandson. "Now, listen well. The lesson you must take from this is never to allow the passion you feel toward your Inferno mate to dishonor her. You must wait until your vows are spoken before a priest. Will you promise this to me?"

"I will."

"And when you have children and grandchildren, you will teach them this lesson?"

"Do you think I wish to have another innocent child suffer what I have?" Rom spoke in a fierce undertone. "When The Inferno strikes a child or grandchild of mine, he or she will wed, willing or not."

"This is vital. For, once you experience The Inferno, it burns within you for the rest of your life."

"Do you think Mamma still loves my father?"

"She loves him to this day, though she will never admit it." *Nonno* rubbed his own palm. "Just as I will love my sweet Nicia from now until the day God delivers me to her, and then for all our time in the hereafter."

"Mamma still rubs her palm, too. I've seen her when she thinks no one is watching."

"Much to Luigi's fury. He adores your mamma. But he knows she does not love him. Not the way she did your father. He will always be second best. That is why he will never accept you." *Nonno* paused, his gaze weighted with regret. "After this visit, you must go your own way, Romero. Though never seeing you again will cause me immense pain, it will be easier for Nicci to walk the road she has chosen, if you were not here as a constant reminder, irritating Luigi."

"I may have something that will help with that." Rom drew the letter from his pocket, handing it to his grandfather. "I've been offered a job as a jewelry designer."

Nonno took the letter and tilted it into the moonlight, studying it for a long moment. His brows drew together. "This company is not affiliated with the Dantes."

"No. It's in America. In San Francisco."

"California?" He gazed at Rom in bewilderment. "Why would you take this job when our Dante relatives have welcomed you as one of their own? Trained you to be a great artisan?"

It was hard to tell his grandfather the truth. But he had to make *Nonno* understand. Rom reached into his other pocket and removed the box containing the ring he'd crafted for Tito. "Tell me what you think of this."

Nonno opened the box, his breath catching in appreciation. *"Com'è bello!* You designed this? Created this? It is magnificent."

Rom nodded. "It's called *L'amore Vero*." He paused, then added. "I am to tell everyone it was made by Donato."

"What's this? That fool make a ring of this quality? He couldn't tell a diamond from a lump of coal."

"No, but at least he's not a bastard. People will trust him. Buy from him. Brag that they've hired him. But someone with my background . . ."

His grandfather closed his eyes. "I'd hoped you would escape the tragedy of your birth. That my cousins would accept you."

"They've accepted me. They're very kind to me." Well, maybe not Donato, but that had more to do with jealousy than anything else. "But I will never become what God intends. Not if I remain the Dantes' secret." He tapped the letter. "In California, no one will know of my stain. If I have anything to say about it, no one will ever know I am a bastard. I can design jewelry without hiding who I am. Someday I will open my own shop. Maybe your cousins will come to accept me then."

"It could happen," *Nonno* said with forced cheer.

"You could travel to America with me."

Nonno shook his head. "My place is with your mamma. Besides, I will not leave my Nicia. When my time comes, I wish to rest beside her." He patted Rom's knee. "You won't be alone, *nipote*. You will take your Inferno bride with you to California. Tell me about her. Where did you meet? Who is her family?"

It was a natural question, though one he'd hoped to avoid. After a momentary hesitation, he admitted, "It's complicated."

Nonno's gaze sharpened. "There can only be one of two explanations for this complication. Either she belongs to another. Or you have no idea who she is or where she lives."

"She belongs to another."

Nonno's dark brows drew together. "She is married?"

"Engaged."

"Ah." His grandfather grimaced. "This is not good. But at least there is time to prevent the marriage from taking place, no?"

"You don't understand. It's Tito's bride."

Nonno closed his eyes and released a gusty sigh. "Unfortunate."

"You know how it is in Santa Lucia. An engagement is as much of a commitment as an actual marriage."

"But it is not an actual marriage. Not yet."

"He's my friend, *Nonno*. For many years he was my *best* friend. He accepted me when most would not."

"It does not matter, Romero," his grandfather argued. "She is not meant for him. In time, he will come to realize this. Better he discovers it before the vows are said, then afterward, would you not agree?"

"Julietta is also unwilling," he confessed.

"But she felt the connection?"

Rom nodded. "I think it frightened her."

"Of course. It would frighten any proper young woman to feel such a powerful desire for a man she's never met before. A man who is not her intended." *Nonno* grinned. "Not that it makes any difference. *La Julietta* can no more resist The Inferno than a nightingale can resist singing."

"You make it sound so simple. But Tito's family is rich and powerful. They will not simply hand over his bride because I ask. Or even because of

The Inferno. Nor will Julietta's family be happy that the bastard of Santa Lucia wishes to marry their daughter. They will cause trouble for us. Even my own family will be opposed to the match."

Nonno brushed the comment aside with a wave of his hand. "The Dantes are rich and powerful, as well. We can handle whatever trouble comes our way."

"I don't know." Rom frowned in concern. "Taking Tito's bride is dishonorable."

"It is not dishonorable to right a wrong. If this young woman has feelings for you, then marrying Tito would be wrong."

Rom shot to his feet and paced beneath the moonlight, his steps ringing against the flagstone pathway. "We've only just met. How can we trust what we're feeling?" Doubts filled him. "What if we're mistaken?"

"The Inferno is never wrong," *Nonno* said simply. "Never."

"Then what must I do?" He turned to face his grandfather. "How do I convince Julietta to break her vow and dishonor her family? She and Tito wed in a week."

"It's very simple." *Nonno* grinned. "You steal her away."

Chapter Three

"Caio, Rom! Come va?"

The call came from the far side of the wall bordering the Ranieri home. Rom glanced up from the herb bed he was weeding, instantly recognizing Tito's voice. His grandfather did, as well, and gave him tacit permission to join his friend with an understanding nod. Rom brushed off his trousers and rinsed his hands beneath the cool water of the garden pump, before exiting through a nearby gate. One look at his boyhood friend and, despite his betrayal, he couldn't help smiling.

"I'm doing well enough, Tito. How are you, old friend?"

"Old." He laughed and slung an arm around Rom's neck, yanking him in for a quick hug and a slap on the back. "And soon to be both older and married, God help me."

"Unbelievable. How did such a thing happen?"

"Caffè first, no? There is a new shop in Santa Lucia that serves a wonderful espresso. *Caffè*

dell'Amore it's called. It will give us a chance to catch up."

"Sounds perfect. Let me grab your engagement ring, and I'll be right with you."

The walk into town gave them the opportunity to exchange the latest gossip and news, though Rom noticed his friend pointedly avoided all mention of Julietta. A short time later, they found the shop just off the piazza and ordered drinks, along with a plate of *bomboloni*.

They decided to eat outside at a small café table where they could enjoy the early morning sunshine. Tito spent the next half hour greeting the steady stream of locals who passed by, all the while devouring both portions of the donuts they'd purchased.

Eventually, he noticed Rom's amusement and grinned. "All this talking and eating, shades of my *babbo,* no? Soon I will be as fat as he is."

Rom went with diplomacy and ignored the latter part of his friend's statement. "One day you'll step into your father's shoes. It's important to develop your own contacts with the people of Santa Lucia."

Tito added a few more sugar cubes to his coffee. "I won't be stepping into my father's shoes if I become a vintner. I'll be far too busy driving your stepfather, Luigi, out of business." He lifted a dark eyebrow, his eyes gleaming with mischievous laughter. "You will not mind, will you?"

Rom shrugged. "There's enough business for everyone." He hesitated, then decided to push the topic of most interest to him. "I understand the vineyard belongs to the family of your bride-to-be."

"Julietta Bianchi, yes. Her poor *babbo* has no sons to help him, only an endless stream of daughters. Taking care of the vines all on his own has become too difficult for him, so he agreed to sell his precious land if I take one of his daughters off his hands."

"It must have been difficult to pick from so many."

Tito made a face. "They gave me no choice. I liked the eldest, but Signora Bianchi insisted it be Julietta. Still, she is a beautiful girl. They tell me she will make a good wife."

"Why wouldn't they let you have the older one?"

"She is meant to become a Bride of Christ." He shook his head in mock sorrow. "More's the pity."

"But—"

Tito swept a hand through the air. "It is done. When you meet Julietta tonight you will see I didn't do too badly for myself." He signaled for the waiter to bring more coffee. "Are you going to show me the ring or keep it a secret until the party?"

Now that the moment had come, he didn't want to give Tito the ring, not when it was meant for Julietta. To allow *his* ring to link *his* woman to another roused an impotent fury he could barely contain. "I have it," he admitted reluctantly. He removed the box from his pocket and set it on the table between them. "I'm to tell you my cousin Donato crafted it."

Tito flipped open the box and inhaled sharply. *"Palle!* That's total bullshit, and you know it. Donato could not have created anything this stunning if he lived to be a hundred."

Rom closed his hands into fists to keep himself from snatching back the box. "I was ordered to tell you Donato is responsible, and so I have." He managed a laugh, though it rang false to his ears. Fortunately, Tito didn't notice anything wrong, or if he did, possibly attributed it to Rom's frustration at having another take credit for his work. "I can't force you to believe me."

"Where did you find this diamond?" Tito studied the flash and fire emanating from the ring. "It's magnificent."

"It's a blue diamond from India. They're very rare, and with the economy so bad, *Nonno's* cousins only bought a few of them. I didn't think they would allow me to have one, let alone cut it." Rom's smile came more naturally this time. "I was very fortunate."

"Your fortune is my fortune." Tito held the ring up toward the sun and shook his head in amazement. He slowly turned it so the rays bounced off the stones, which sparkled with a deep inner radiance. "Of course, I'm paying well for it."

Rom sat back, reluctant to accept praise for a ring he would have been delighted to see on any finger other than Julietta's. He'd designed it with love, care, and attention to detail. He suspected that, more than anything, had convinced the patriarch of Dantes Jewelry to allow him to fashion the ring. The arguments had raged for weeks among the various family members, with Donato among the fiercest debaters, before Rom had received permission to work on the commission. But in the end, he'd won, and *L'amore Vero* was his greatest accomplishment to date.

He'd used the blue diamond for the centerpiece, long believing diamonds came from the flaming heart of the earth and were physical representations of its love. They were his preferred choice for engagement and wedding rings above all other stones. Around one side of the ring, he'd set a swirl of tiny diamonds, around the other side, a swirl of sapphires. The two swirls met at the diamond, to surround and merge and overlap, symbolizing the joining and ultimate union of man and woman. It expressed his feelings toward love and marriage. *L'amore Vero*. True love. The most sacred type of marriage.

Tito carefully pocketed the ring. "You are seriously talented, Rom. There's something about your designs that lifts them above mere jewelry." He paused while he thought it through, sipping his coffee. "If a dozen rings were set before me, I could pick out the one you had made. Hell, I could single out yours even if there were a hundred rings from which to choose. I think I would recognize them anywhere."

Rom flinched. He'd designed this ring for Tito's marriage to Julietta, a woman he intended to steal away. Guilt threatened to overwhelm him, and a confession trembled on the tip of his tongue, fighting for escape. He ruthlessly bit it back. "You humble me, Tito."

His friend grinned. "I hope someday you will be able to say the same about my wines. One sip and you will know it is a Rossi."

Relieved the moment for confession had passed, Rom lifted his cup of coffee and tapped it against Tito's. "*Salute*. May we both find success in our endeavors."

"And may we both live our dreams."

Julietta stood beside her fiancé beneath the widespread embrace of a stand of orange trees bordering the Rossi villa, greeting the final guests arriving for their engagement party. Petals rained down, much as they had the day before when she and Rom—

She ruthlessly broke off the thought. It was time to put yesterday's fantasies aside and accept the role she'd been given.

Bride.

Wife.

Mother.

Chattel.

She'd been bought and sold as surely as the Bianchi vineyards. Or perhaps it would be more accurate to say, *she* represented the vineyards, providing a conduit connecting land to owner. Even her green dress and the wreath of poppies, mustard, nuts, and oak twigs in her hair announced the primary duty she'd be expected to fulfill, bearing her husband a child, preferably a son.

Tito leaned in to speak quietly in her ear. "I have something for you." Before she had an opportunity to question him, he took her hand in his and slipped a ring on her finger. It stuck at her second knuckle and, to her embarrassment, took some wiggling to get on. "I had intended to give this to you sooner, but I only just received it. Obviously, we'll get it resized."

She stared at the ring, a stunning representation of her commitment to Tito. It was one more anchor binding her, the weight it represented infinitely greater than the weight on her finger. Honesty compelled her to concede it was also the most beautiful piece of jewelry she'd ever seen. It spoke to her, whispering an unwanted truth about love and marriage. Tito hadn't gifted her with a ring of convenience for a marriage of convenience, but a ring meant for a fairy tale type love affair. It should have come from a groom madly in love with his bride, and she with him, a symbol of the type of love that transcended the ordinary, that became the stuff of legends.

This ring was meant for true love.

"Do you like it?" Tito asked quietly.

She nodded, her throat tightening with emotion. How could she not? "It's spectacular," she whispered.

"I asked one of my best friends to design it specially for you."

"You did?"

She searched his expression, hunting for some sign his feelings for her ran deeper than his desire for her family's land. Why couldn't she love this man? He was good and kind and generous. He'd be so easy to love, if not for Rom. Maybe if she tried, really tried, she could do what her family expected. Be an obedient daughter. Be a good wife. Be a loving mother to her children.

Once again, the image of a forked path rose before her. The well-trod road to the right led to Tito, the "ideal" husband. The safe husband. The husband who would provide for her and her children. It was a path repeatedly chosen by women throughout the centuries, and for a very good reason. He was the sort of man who would ensure the survival of his family. How could she reject that?

She shook her head. She couldn't. As of tonight, she'd commit herself to taking that course, as well. And never again would she glance toward her other option, that delicious pathway that tempted her beyond reason.

She smiled at Tito, the first genuine smile she'd offered all day. "*Grazie*. That was very thoughtful of you. Please thank your friend for me."

"Thank him yourself. Here he is now."

Abrupt awareness hit, a blinding flash that caused Julietta's breath to quicken and her blood to heat. She knew who stood there without even looking. She could feel the connection centered in her palm and the way it radiated throughout every part of her. It filled her with a desperate yearning, a need to be part of him. To turn and forge a connection, even if only through their joined hands. Her palm itched, and she fisted her hand to keep from rubbing at the tantalizing burn centered there. Slowly, she faced Rom. Time seemed to slow, the air to thicken. From a great distance she heard him speak.

"It's a pleasure to meet you, Signorina Bianchi."

"Please," she managed to say. "Call me Julietta."

"Julietta."

The way he said her name sent shivers down her spine, the timbre of his voice resonating in a way she'd never experienced before. She wanted him to keep talking, to say her name over and over. Not that he did. He took her hand in his and leaned in, kissing first one cheek and then the other.

She ached to turn her head the necessary few inches so his mouth collided with hers, instead of with her cheek. Did he sense her reaction, sense how hard she fought to control it? He must have, since she trembled beneath his touch, the desperate hitch in her breath clearly audible. She prayed no one else noticed anything amiss, especially Tito.

She slanted her fiancé a swift look from beneath her lashes. He stood beside her, tall and straight and proud. In a purely conventional sense, he was far better-looking than Rom. But he held none of the appeal. He faded into obscurity in comparison to his friend. And when he smiled at her, she felt nothing at all.

No, that wasn't true. She felt a kinship, but more in line with how she might react toward a friend or relative. Certainly not what she'd hoped to feel for her husband. And it didn't begin to compare to what she experienced with Rom.

Please, God, don't let Tito notice my attraction to his friend!

She deliberately shifted closer to the man she'd promised to marry. He took her hand in his, breaking her physical link to his friend, and gave it a quick squeeze. Every instinct she possessed urged her to snatch her hand free. Instead, she returned his squeeze before addressing Rom.

"You made my engagement ring?"

He nodded, and she could see the conflicted emotions sweep across his face. Pride. Regret. Yearning. "I did. Do you like it?"

Tears filled her eyes, and she struggled to express her reaction to his creation. It was the perfect ring, given to her by the wrong man. If only Rom had been the one to slip it on to her finger. If only... "Your ring, it's—" To her horror her voice broke.

Tito wrapped an arm around her. "What's wrong, *cucciola mia?*"

"I'm sorry. I don't know what's gotten into me." She fought to steady her breathing. "It's nothing. Nothing at all."

"It's probably the crush of people. Understandable. Maybe a glass of wine will help." He glanced at Rom. "Would you stay with Julietta while I get her a drink?"

"Of course."

"It's not necessary. I just need a moment," Julietta started to say. But Tito had already gone.

She stood unmoving, not daring to look at Rom, not when every thought and emotion must be emblazoned across her face. She didn't even dare take a step farther away from him, in case he realized just how much his presence threatened to overpower her. "What are you doing here?" she whispered.

"I'm here for your wedding."

"And to give Tito my engagement ring." She twisted her hands together, the ring a painful weight. "I wish you'd never come."

"That's not true."

Then he did the unthinkable. He captured her hand in his, linking fingers so their palms melded. Instantly, The Inferno sparked, and the emotions she'd fought so hard to suppress flared to life. They seemed to sink inward, deepening and becoming more and more part of her with each beat of her heart.

"You want me every bit as much as I want you. This wedding to Tito, it's wrong. Call it off, Julietta, while there's still time."

She lowered her voice to a mere whisper of sound. "My parents won't let me. You must realize that. They need the money Tito brings to the marriage."

"He'll buy the vineyards even if you're not part of the deal."

If only it were possible. If only it were that simple. She shook her head. "After Tito bought the vineyards, that would be the end of it. I have seven other sisters. If he becomes their brother, he'll look after them. Provide for them, if necessary."

"Their husbands can provide for them. Or better yet, let one of them marry Tito. What about Serena?"

He was destroying her, inch by inch. How could she do what he suggested when it meant sacrificing her family in exchange for her own happiness? Maybe if she kept them in mind it would help control the raging demand of The Inferno. Maybe.

"Serena has been promised to the church in gratitude for seeing us safely through the war."

"A shame."

Rom drew Julietta closer. Just a step, but a dangerous one. The uniqueness of his scent tantalized her, the earthy, irresistible perfume distinct to him. Is this what the scientists meant by chemistry? It seemed so basic to her, almost primal, twining through her and connecting them in some fundamental way. His essence branded her, stamped itself on all her senses. She wanted to inhale him. Taste him. Touch every masculine inch of him.

He must have picked up on something similar, because he inhaled deeply, and his pupils dilated, darkness expanding into the ring of antique gold. *"Dio mio,* what is that perfume you're wearing?"

She swallowed a soft moan. "I'm not wearing any perfume. Are you?"

"Never."

She suspected as much. Over Rom's shoulder she saw Tito approaching. "You have to let me go."

"Never," he repeated.

"Tito's coming. Please, let go of my hand."

She dared to glance around, praying no one had noticed anything unusual. Music and laughter flowed around them. It seemed as though all of Santa Lucia had invaded the Rossis' spacious home and garden. The guests were busy eating and celebrating, paying far more attention to the tables groaning beneath the weight of food than to the bride-to-be, half-hidden by Rom's broad shoulders and the shadowy embrace of an orange tree. Only Serena seemed to have any awareness that something was amiss. She lifted an eyebrow, then made a naughty girl gesture. Julietta shook her head, but her reaction came too late. Her sister had already vanished into a crowd of revelers.

Rom took a step back, reluctantly releasing her hand just as Tito joined them. He carried a large glass of wine, and she closed her eyes, torn between relief and regret. "How's our nervous bride?" he asked.

"I'm fine," she insisted.

"Drink." He slapped Rom on the shoulder. "Thanks for looking after her, *mio amico.*"

She accepted the proffered glass with a self-conscious smile and took a sip. It was one of her family's labels, a rustic, full-bodied Sangiovese, highlighted with dark chocolate and smoke flavors. It did help steady her. More, it helped remind her of her duties and responsibilities, none of which included a romantic interlude with her fiancé's best friend.

"Thank you. I feel much better now."

Tito held out his hand. "Come. Let's take a walk while you drink your wine. There are too many people here. You probably need a break from all the noise."

Without a choice, she allowed Tito to lead her away from Rom and into the shadow-draped seclusion of the orange grove that bordered the garden. A moon, just shy of full, offered a rough footpath of scattered light. Julietta searched frantically for a topic of conversation. Heaven help her, they weren't even married yet, and they'd already run out of things to say to one another.

"Alone at last," Tito murmured.

She caught an odd intonation beneath the words and stumbled. Instantly, Tito wrapped an arm around her, drawing her close. "Be careful, *passerotta*. I wouldn't want my bride walking down the aisle on crutches."

Julietta stilled, fighting the instinctive urge to push him away. "First you call me a puppy, now a sparrow. Is that how you see me?"

He slid his fingers into her hair and tipped her face toward his. "You're so small and delicate." He sighed with something that sounded like regret. "So young."

"You prefer your women a bit more—" She thought of Serena. "Earthy?"

He shrugged. "I prefer women however they come."

The rumors she'd heard since coming to Santa Lucia taunted her. She'd never have had the nerve to address them, if not for Rom. If not for wishing the man she married would love her the way another did.

"And will you continue to prefer women 'however they come' after we're married?" she dared to ask.

The amusement faded from his expression, replaced by a sternness he'd never revealed before. "That is not an appropriate question to ask."

Wasn't it? A woman's certainty filled her. If it were Rom standing before her, the question would never have to be asked. She'd already know the answer. He'd never cheat on her. But that same conviction didn't extend to Tito. "I think knowing whether or not my fiancé intends to stay faithful to his wedding vows is a very appropriate question to ask."

"Very well." He paused. "I suppose that depends on you."

She pulled back. "What do you mean?" To her alarm, his hold tightened, and he tugged her close again. "What are you doing?"

"I mean that a husband who is fortunate enough to have a passionate wife has a far easier time remaining faithful than one who discovers his marriage bed is cold and barren." He lowered his head and feathered a kiss across her cheek. "And to answer your other question, what I'm doing is discovering whether my bride is one of fire. Or of ice."

Then Tito kissed her. Her wineglass tumbled from her hand, shattering on a rock at her feet. Blood-red wine splattered across her legs and the hem of her dress. This was a far different kiss from any he'd offered before. This one took possession of her mouth, demanding rather than asking. Invading instead of entreating. He forced an entrance, his breath sour with beer, the flavor in conflict with the wine she'd been drinking. The few occasions he'd kissed her before, she hadn't felt much of anything, neither pleasure nor antipathy.

This time, revulsion swept through her. His touch repelled her, as did his kiss. He didn't have the right to make love to her, not when she belonged to another. How could she have ever thought differently?

He held her anchored against him with one arm banded around her waist. The other slipped between them, his hand coasting across her breast. He fumbled with the neckline of her bodice, shoving aside the collar of her dress. When Rom had touched her like this, she'd tumbled into the sweet grass with him and allowed him a far greater intimacy than Tito was attempting. But this was wrong, so horribly wrong. Wrenching her mouth from his, she silently fought him, a hiccup of panic bubbling in her throat.

Tito groaned impatiently. "Come on, Julietta. It's no big deal. I just want to make love to my fiancée. Just a little kissing." He thrust his hand into the bodice of her dress and cupped her breast. "And maybe a little touching."

"No!" She fought harder, frantic at the idea of any man other than Rom putting his hands on her. "Don't touch me."

Her dress ripped, the sound of rending cloth a sharp note of discord against the sleepy nighttime murmurs surrounding them. Tito froze, his grasp loosening. It gave her the opportunity she needed. She shoved him away, scrubbing the back of her hand across her lips and spitting the taste of him from her mouth.

The instant she had, she froze, realizing what she'd done. The breath caught in her throat, and she stared at him in distress. Slowly, she pulled the torn edges of her dress across her breasts, terrified of what he'd do to her for offending him so. He returned her gaze, his dark eyes stony and his expression carved into deep lines of insult. But he didn't react with the anger she'd anticipated. Instead he gathered himself with a calm dignity that filled her with shame.

"So it'll be ice. I must admit, I'm disappointed." He took a step back. "Not that it changes anything. Our marriage was always about gain. I gain a vineyard. You gain a rich husband. But a word of advice, *amore*. You might not want to show your distaste quite so clearly. You'll find your husband is far more cooperative if you preserve the illusion you can actually stomach his touch." And with that, he walked away.

Julietta lifted a shaking hand to her mouth. What had she done? And how could she undo it? She shook her head. It wasn't possible. Tito would never forgive her for her actions. And even if he did, the idea of his putting his hands on her ever again filled her with horror. Tears burned her eyes.

How could she possibly marry a man who repulsed her? And yet, how could she refuse to marry him when her family's welfare was at stake? She stared in the direction Tito had taken—toward the lights and music of their engagement party. Turning, she fled in the opposite direction.

Chapter Four

Tito stormed back toward the party with one goal in mind. To get blinding, stupid, fall-down drunk. If it weren't for the vineyards, he'd put an end to the farce of his engagement and follow in his father's footsteps. But ever since he'd been a toddler and first discovered the wonder of a new plant erupting from the soil as if by magic, he'd known he possessed the heart of a farmer, rather than that of an entrepreneur. The land and its bounty drew him. And not just any crop would do.

Grapes called to him.

It had taken him years to convince his family he could increase their fortunes by adding a vineyard to their other business concerns. It had taken even longer for Tito to persuade his stubborn father that he was the best man to run the new venture. Finding the perfect vineyard had been nothing short of a miracle. And if all it took to acquire the vineyard was some money and a proposal of marriage, then, by God, that's what he'd do. Anything, if it gave him his dream.

So he wouldn't enjoy passion in his marriage bed the way he'd hoped. Many men found satisfaction elsewhere. He'd simply join their ranks. He reached the outskirts of the party and attached himself to a group of old men who were passing around a bottle. Not wine or beer, but something far more potent. Just what he needed.

Julietta's sister Serena approached before he'd taken more than a sip or two. "Would you like a drink?" he offered, certain she'd refuse.

She surprised him by accepting, tossing back the liquor in a way that left him grinning. She handled it with amazing aplomb for an entire five seconds before choking. "What is that?" she wheezed.

"I'm not sure, but it's guaranteed to grow hair on your chest."

Her eyes widened, and then she laughed. "Now you tell me." She linked arms with him and drew him away from the men—and the bottle. "I gather you and Julietta had a fight?"

"Why do you say that?"

She shot him a chiding look. "Why else would you drown your sorrows, while my sister is nowhere to be seen? Would you like to talk about it?"

"Practicing to be a nun already, are you? Offering comfort and counsel to the needy?"

She pinched his arm. "Don't be an idiot. Despite what my family's wishes, I'm not cut out for the life."

They skirted the edge of the party and stood beside a gate leading to his mother's vegetable garden. It was far from the noise of the party, and a sultry darkness dwelled within, the air sweetened by the scent of growing plants. Serena nudged open the gate with a rounded hip and stepped into the garden. The night wrapped her in a gentle embrace that smudged the her contours. He could see her movements, the graceful flutter and sway so unique to a woman. But her outline lacked definition, adding a hint of mystery to the moment.

"So, what happened with my sister?" Her voice drifted to him, ensnaring him and pulling him deeper into the fertile pocket of ripening fruit and vegetables. "Why did you fight?"

"It was my fault," he conceded. He'd rushed Julietta. Though he doubted going slow with that one would have made the least difference, not when his touch clearly repelled her.

"Your fault?" Serena sounded startled. She swung around to face him, her fists planted on her ample hips. He caught the piercing flash of her eyes, cutting through the darkness. "What did you do to her, Tito Rossi?"

He could never say what insanity seized him. He couldn't even blame it on too much drink since he'd barely enjoyed a sip or two of the potent brew. Maybe it was the scent of growing vegetation, bursting with the lush, intoxicating nectar of life. "Why don't I show you?" he suggested.

He planted his hands on her hips and tugged her close. To his surprise, she didn't protest but allowed him to fit her body to his. She was taller than Julietta and more full-figured, her curves sweetly generous. She stared at him with eyes as calm and serene as her name. He hesitated, recalling his fiancée's reaction to his touch.

She tilted her head to one side. "You fought about a simple embrace?" she asked.

"No." Her lips tempted him. They were like the rest of her, round and plump and welcoming. More than anything, he wanted to experience them, see if they tasted as delicious as they appeared. "We fought over this."

He gave into temptation and kissed her, taking it slow and easy. Not that he needed to. She responded instantly, her lips parting beneath his, welcoming him inward. It couldn't have been any more different from what he'd experienced earlier.

Where before he'd met ice, now he found fire. Where before he'd struck resistance, now he discovered welcome. Her arms slid around his neck and tightened, pulling him closer, while her tongue dueled with his. Desire swept through him, exploding in a way he'd never dreamed possible. He wanted this woman with a passion every bit as great as his passion for the land. Maybe more.

He didn't know how long the moment would have continued if someone hadn't approached from the direction of the party, singing in a low, off-key baritone. Serena stiffened, dragging her mouth from his. With a sigh of regret, Tito released her.

"I'm sorry," she said. Her hands slid a path of reluctant retreat across his chest. "I shouldn't have let that happen."

"It wasn't your fault." He covered her hands with his, holding them against his heart for a brief moment before releasing her. "I had too much to drink."

Though he no longer touched her, she continued to stand close enough to stoke the embers of their embrace. "Are you going to tell Julietta what happened between us?"

Would his fiancée even care that he'd made love to her sister? "I don't think that would be wise, do you?"

Serena shook her head. "Probably not." She searched his expression, though he suspected the night concealed it from her—*grazie a Dio*—since it would have given away far too much. "I think she'd call off the engagement."

"I can't let that happen." His hands dropped briefly to her shoulders, his touch communicating an underlying urgency. "I asked for your hand first, did your father tell you?"

Serena shook her head and tears glittered in her eyes. "They've promised me to the church," she confessed in a low voice. "Though it is not the path I would take if given the choice."

"That's what I was told. Nor does it change the bottom line for me." He forced himself to say the hurtful words, even though they wounded him every bit as much as Serena. "I want your family's vineyard. And marrying your sister is the only way I'll get it."

She didn't debate the issue. She simply nodded, accepting the truth of his statement. But he noticed she surreptitiously wiped away a tear. That, more than anything, threatened to gut him. "I should return before anyone misses me."

They waited until the man passed by, heading for the main road. The instant silence blanketed the garden, Serena crossed to the gate. She paused there, perhaps to gather in a final breath of what might have been. Tito followed. Unable to resist, he slid his hand along the supple length of her spine and whispered, "It should have been you."

Rom frowned in concern. Where the hell was Julietta? Tito had returned twenty minutes ago without her, looking thoroughly pissed, before disappearing again. But she hadn't rejoined the party. Maybe he should track her down, just to be on the safe side.

Calling himself every sort of idiot for involving himself in business that was none of his concern—even if his heart told him something far different—he headed into the orange grove. It took a moment for his eyes to adjust to the darkness, the moonlight lending some assistance. About a hundred meters into the grove the glitter of glass caught his eye, and he found the broken shards of the wineglass she'd been carrying.

"Julietta?" he called, concern giving a sharp edge to his voice.

He heard a movement a little deeper into the grove and followed the sound. He found her a short distance away, curled up at the base of an orange tree, crying.

"Julietta?" He sprinted to her side and crouched beside her. Her head jerked up at the sound of his voice, and moonlight struck her face. Tears tracked a silvery path along her cheeks, and the wreath she wore in her hair had slipped to one side. "What happened? What did that bastard do to you?" he demanded.

"Nothing." She drew away from him, sitting a little straighter, and the bodice of her dress slipped from one shoulder. Her breath hitched in her lungs, and she fumbled with the torn material, attempting to cover her breast. "It was nothing."

He saw red, fury scorching him with white-hot flames. "That isn't nothing." He helped her adjust her dress, keeping his touch cautious and soothing. "I swear, I'll kill that *figlio di puttana*."

She shook her head. "No. No," she repeated, more forcefully. "He didn't do anything wrong. He just kissed me. I overreacted."

Rom clenched his teeth, fighting to control the seething fury that gripped him. She was engaged to Tito, he reminded himself. His friend had every right to kiss her. Hell, in another week, he'd have the right to do far more than demand a kiss. He shoved the image aside, focusing instead on Julietta and her needs.

"You can't go back to the party like that."

"Maybe you could find Serena." Julietta made a helpless, fluttery gesture. "She can explain to the guests. Make my excuses. Tell them I'm not well or something."

Rom shook his head. "I don't want to leave you alone in the orchard. I'll get you home, first, then let Serena know you're not well."

She gripped his arm. "Promise me you won't say anything to Tito. That you won't argue with him about this."

He took a moment to consider. Every instinct he possessed urged him to confront his friend, to go after him for hurting Julietta. But how would that help? If anything, it might cause irreparable harm. "What happened when he kissed you?" He asked the question reluctantly, knowing her answer would influence his decision. "How did your dress get torn?"

He didn't think she'd respond. After a brief second, she closed her eyes and shuddered. "He kissed me."

"But he's kissed you before." Rom surveyed her dress with grim distaste. "I hope not this roughly."

"He has kissed me before. And those other times weren't bad. I mean, it wasn't like when you and I—"

She broke off and glanced at him, her gaze full of the memories from the times they'd been together. Everything about her softened, radiating a feminine warmth that twined around and through him. Drew him toward her and urged him to take her in his arms again.

He couldn't resist teasing. "Like when you and I . . . *what?*"

"It wasn't like when we kissed," she confessed in a low voice. A frown creased her brow. "It didn't repulse me before. But this time I found it disgusting."

He forced himself to ignore his baser desires and focus instead on Julietta and her needs. "Tito's kisses didn't repulse you until tonight?" A combination of satisfaction and regret coursed through him. "Is this the first time he's kissed you since you and I met?"

Julietta nodded. "And when he did, I hated it. It wasn't his fault," she hastened to add. "We're to be married and he wanted—" She broke off self-consciously.

Rom schooled himself to calmness. Anger wouldn't help the situation. Nor did he have the right to protect her from Tito. At least, not yet. "He wanted to touch you."

She shot him a direct look. "Yes. The same way you touched me. With you, I didn't mind."

Rom lifted an eyebrow. "Didn't mind?"

A hint of a smile chased away the last of her tears. "Not even a little."

"Perhaps you enjoyed it?" he pressed.

Her smile grew, taking on a mischievous slant. "Perhaps. Perhaps I enjoyed it a lot." Then her smile faded. "But with Tito it felt wrong. I panicked, and we struggled for a moment." She released a tired sigh. "That's when my dress ripped."

She dragged the ruined wreath from her hair and tossed it aside. Stray sprigs of yellow flowering mustard and a few red poppies remained snared in her wayward curls, along with a twig or two of oak. Captured within the moon's embrace, she looked like a tattered wood nymph.

Rom carefully untangled one of the twigs and, unable to help himself, wound the spill of curls around his hand. With a sigh of pleasure, she followed the gentle tug and slipped into his arms, nestling against him. His arms closed tight around her, and he wrapped her in a protective hold. She fit against him with such perfection, with such overwhelming "rightness." No wonder she'd reacted the way she had to Tito's embrace. He'd react the same way if another woman touched him with a lover's caress. He'd find it abhorrent. Sacrilegious.

"You're right, *amata mia,*" Rom said quietly. He pressed a kiss to the crown of her head and inhaled the scent of her, drawing it in and making it as much a part of him as his own breath. Everything about her marked him, her essence imprinting on each of his senses. "None of this is Tito's fault."

"It's because of The Inferno, isn't it?" She dropped her gaze to her hand and rubbed a spot in the middle of her palm, the same spot he'd caught himself rubbing. "I didn't believe you before. When we first met, and you told me we were soul mates and all that nonsense about The Inferno, I thought you made it up in order to seduce me."

"Perhaps, if I were the type of man to seduce innocent women." But he wasn't, not when he'd watched his mother suffer from the consequences of such an act. "What changed your mind about me?"

"This." She held out her hand, and he took it in his, pressing a kiss into the heart of her palm. "I felt it from the moment we first touched, just as I still feel it now. I can feel *you*. And that feeling is in my blood and in my bones. It races through me with every single beat of my heart. It terrifies me until I listen to what it's saying."

"And what is it saying?" he asked tenderly.

"To trust you."

His arms tightened around her, and he closed his eyes, tipping his head against the rough bark of the orange tree at his back. "You humble me with your faith. I swear I'll do everything in my power to deserve it."

Her mouth brushed his jawline, the touch as soft and fleeting as the sweep of a butterfly's wings. "Well, at least I know you're not trying to seduce me."

His laugh held a painful edge. "Don't make me out to be a saint, Julietta. That's one accusation no one's ever leveled at me." He traced her torn bodice with his fingertip. "And I am trying to seduce you. It's all I've thought about since we first met. It's taking every ounce of self-control to keep from ripping this the rest of the way off and making you mine in the most basic and natural way possible."

Her heartbeat fluttered beneath his fingers. One look reassured him the quickening of her pulse didn't come from fear, but desire. He could see it in her heated gaze, watch the sweep of it shift her expression from concerned to ardent. Considering what had just happened with Tito, Rom wouldn't have been surprised if she distanced herself from him. Instead, she shifted even closer.

"Okay, maybe you are trying to seduce me. But that's not all you want from me. I realize that now." Her hand covered his. "Just as I know you won't do anything to dishonor me."

His amusement faded, and pain sliced through him. "No, I'd never do that. How could I, when I know how my mother has suffered because of one passionate mistake? She's spent a lifetime of penitence paying for a single night of love. And while both the man and woman may lose their honor, a woman loses far more than that, especially when there are consequences."

"You mean a baby." Julietta captured his face between her soft hands, gazing at him with eyes deep and dark and filled with a woman's perception. "It isn't just the man and woman who suffer. You're the consequence. You suffered, as well. You've never been accepted for yourself, have you?"

He shook his head, her sensitivity unnerving. No one had ever seen inside him with as much clarity as she possessed. It stripped him of all protection, cut through all barriers, and exposed his true self at the core, both good and bad.

"I've always been the bastard of Santa Lucia. I'm both the reason men warn their daughters about certain men. And the type of man fathers keep their daughters hidden from." He whispered the admission, not realizing until that moment how deep the wound went, or how much it had festered through the years. "I'm the last to be hired for a job. The first to be suspected of any mischief or theft or villainy. I'm the man who's watched with constant suspicion. I was born without honor and therefore must work to earn even the most grudging respect."

"Even in Florence?"

"It's easier there," he conceded. "My relatives are more forgiving, but only up to a point."

"And what point is that?"

"They respect me and my talent. But they'll never allow their customers to know I'm the one who crafted their jewelry. That person must have an impeccable reputation so the elite of Florence will trust and favor us with their patronage."

She stared in distress. "They told you this?"

He nodded. "Before I left for Santa Lucia. I was told that while I may design and fashion Dante jewelry, I must give my cousin Donato credit for every piece I create, including your engagement ring."

"You sound so matter-of-fact about it," she marveled. "Aren't you angry?"

"Not angry." He hesitated, thinking about the letter from San Francisco offering him the opportunity for a new life, and chose his words with care. "Determined. I'm determined to change my circumstances."

She frowned over his words. "I never considered the possibility of changing my circumstances. I've always accepted the direction I've been told to take, trusting my parents to know what's best for me." She caught her lower lip between her teeth, considering such a wondrous possibility. "It will be incredibly difficult to pick a different path at this point."

"Yes, it will," he limited himself to saying.

He refused to force her decision, no matter how desperately he might wish to. It was her life. And though he believed they belonged together, were meant for one another, the final choice had to be hers. Forging a new life in a new country wouldn't be easy—especially since he hadn't even told her about the possibility of moving to America. They both needed to be totally committed to each other and to whatever direction they took from this point on.

Rom brushed her hair from her face and feathered a kiss across her mouth. Her lips clung and parted beneath his with a natural eagerness that humbled him. He anticipated reticence, especially after the incident with Tito. Instead, he encountered unstinting generosity. He took it slow, loath to do anything to alarm or panic her. Not that she acted the least alarmed or panicked. In fact, she wriggled closer with unmistakable eagerness and returned his kisses with a sweet intensity that threatened his sanity.

Unable to resist, he swept aside the ruined pieces of her bodice to uncover the softness within. He wanted to erase all memory of Tito's touch. To replace it with his own. To exchange misery for joy. She had the most perfect breasts he'd ever seen, round and plump and succulent as a ripe peach, tipped with nipples as tasty as the sweetest spring berries. She tilted her head back so her hair rained across her shoulders to the ground, surrounding them in a carpet of curls.

At the first touch of his mouth, Julietta sighed in pleasure. Her hands forked into his hair, and she held him close. She smelled so amazing, like a flower whose scent drove him wild, its petals softer than anything he'd ever felt before. She shifted against him, and he soothed her with a gentle stroke to her waist and hip. Her dress rode high on her legs, and he allowed his fingertips to drift across skin like satin. Her thighs parted ever so slightly, and he followed the warmth to its core.

Soft cotton covered her, and that stopped him. There was something so innocent about cotton, as innocent as the woman he held. *Nonno's* warning returned, along with the memory of all his mother had suffered as a result of allowing The Inferno to sweep aside common sense and reason. Gently, he smoothed her dress over her legs and tugged the edges of her bodice together to cover her breasts.

"I promised I wouldn't dishonor you, and yet, that's what I'm on the verge of doing." He shifted her to one side in order to give them both some breathing space. The torn neckline of her dress gaped, exposing the fragile length of her collarbone and the sweet curve of her breast. "We need to stop now before it's too late."

"It's already too late." Serena stepped from shadow into moonlight. "Get away from my sister, you bastard. Before I scream the place down."

Chapter Five

"Serena!" Julietta shot to her feet. "What are you doing here?"

"Attempting to track you down before anyone notices you're missing. And what do I find?" She pointed an accusing finger in Rom's direction. "You, cheating on Tito with this one."

Julietta held out a beseeching hand. "You don't understand."

"You're right. I don't." Resentment crept into Serena's voice, taking on a darkness that matched the shadow-draped night. "Tito is offering you the perfect life. He's handsome. Wealthy. He'll take care of our family. *Che ti passa per la testa?* What's the matter with you? What more could you possibly want?"

"Love," Julietta instantly replied.

Serena groaned. *"Ma va!* You really have lost your mind."

"Is it crazy to want a man who loves me?" She sensed Rom's approach, providing a powerful bulwark at her back. She leaned against his strength, fumbling to hold her ripped dress in place. "I don't love Tito, any more than he loves me. I love Rom."

Serena frowned. "What happened to your dress?" She gasped, her gaze shifting to Rom, outrage adding fuel to her fury. "Did he do that to you?"

"Don't be ridiculous. Of course, he didn't."

"I don't believe you. He was trying to take advantage of you. To—"

"It was Tito," Julietta interrupted, her voice unnaturally loud within the quiet confines of the orange grove. "Tito tried to take advantage of me. Tito ripped my dress."

Serena shook her head. "No. No, he wouldn't do that."

"Not deliberately," she conceded. "If I hadn't fought him, my dress wouldn't have gotten ripped, so I guess it wasn't totally his fault."

"So, that's what Tito meant when—" Serena broke off, and Julietta couldn't help but wonder what she'd intended to say. She gestured toward Rom. "And this one? Don't pretend you weren't cheating on Tito with him. I saw enough to know better."

Rom stepped in at that point, taking charge with a natural authority. "This isn't the time to discuss it. Serena, please tell everyone Julietta isn't feeling well and has left. I'll make sure your sister gets safely home."

Serena folded her arms across her chest. "I think I'd better take my sister home while you tell everyone we've left."

Julietta shook her head. "No." She didn't often stand up to her older sister. She tended to be the one who went along with others' needs and desires, the easygoing sister. Until Rom. Until The Inferno had struck. Until she'd found something worth the fight. Now she refused to bend. Now she'd stand strong. "Rom will take me. Please offer my apologies to everyone."

Without another word, she slipped her hand in Rom's and headed in the direction of the Rossis' cottage. "You're making a mistake," Serena called after her.

"It's my mistake to make," she whispered, even though her sister couldn't hear.

But Rom did. "Is it a mistake?"

She glanced down at their joined hands and shook her head. "It doesn't feel like one."

"Will she tell the others?"

Julietta shrugged. "I hope not. But it's a possibility. There's . . ." She chose her words with care. "There's a lot at stake, and she might feel the family's well-being is more important than keeping our secret."

"I'd rather be up front about it. Tell our families and Tito the truth."

"And what do you think will happen if we do?" she argued. "My family will lock me away until the wedding. Yours will insist you return to Florence. And your friendship with Tito will be destroyed."

"My friendship with Tito was destroyed the moment I saw you. The instant I touched you."

She didn't debate the point. How could she when he spoke the truth? "How is it possible that one man's touch can be so wrong and another's so perfect?"

Rom paused within sight of the Rossi cottage and pulled Julietta into a loose embrace. "If it had been my choice, I'd never have fallen in love with you." His statement held a touch of apology. "You're my best friend's fiancée."

"It could have been worse," she insisted quietly. "I could have already been married to Tito. Or what if I'd never become engaged to him at all? We're from different worlds. My village is several hours away from yours. If not for my engagement, we might never have met."

"Perhaps that's part of The Inferno's blessing. It found a way to bring us together when we'd never have met under normal circumstances."

Julietta frowned. "This Inferno, it's the reason I hated Tito kissing me, when it never bothered me before. That's why I fought him, isn't it?"

"Probably." He traced the edge of her torn dress, from her collarbone to the upper curve of her breast. "You seem so fragile. So vulnerable. I don't dare touch you again, not even to reassure you."

Julietta smiled. "I'm not all that fragile. I promise I won't break. But I don't dare touch you, either. I'm not strong enough to stop."

"You realize you can't go through with this marriage, don't you?"

"I thought I could, until . . ." She shuddered. *"Dio mi perdoni*, what am I going to do? It will destroy my family if I refuse to marry Tito."

"Your family will survive. Either Tito will buy the vineyard outright, or he'll choose one of your other sisters instead." He attempted to joke. "Maybe no one's bothered to tell you, but arranged marriages are a thing of the past."

Her laugh held more pain than amusement. "Not in Santa Lucia. Not in my village, either. And not when it comes to the Bianchi family." She spoke with difficulty. "My parents have always done everything within their power to keep my family safe, even during the war when safety had more to do with luck than anything else. Is it any wonder I trust them to make wise decisions on my behalf?"

"Do they not allow their daughters to marry for love?" he asked gently.

"Yes, but only if love coincides with more practical concerns."

Rom simply nodded. "My friends in Florence might laugh at the old-fashioned, rustic ways of village life. But certain traditions are slow to change. This is one of them." He fell silent for a moment, then asked, "Even if Tito weren't in the picture, they'd never agree to a marriage between us, would they?"

She hesitated for a mere second before shaking her head, not bothering to prevaricate. Rom wouldn't appreciate her giving him anything but the straight, unvarnished truth. "No."

"Because I'm a bastard."

"Yes," she whispered.

He took her hand in his and allowed their palms to lock together. "Not to mention the Dante family's curse. They probably wouldn't appreciate dealing with that, any more than you do."

She looked at him with undisguised curiosity, combined with a hint of compassion. "Do you really consider The Inferno a curse rather than a blessing?"

He shrugged. "I suppose it's two sides of the same coin. It just depends which side comes up when the coin is flipped. Whatever this is, it hasn't given you any more of a choice than your parents insisting you marry Tito. The Inferno drives you into my arms, whereas your parents force you to the altar to wed a man you don't love. You didn't ask for this marriage or for The Inferno. And if you had, you probably wouldn't have agreed to either one."

"I'm not sure." Her brows drew together, and her gaze turned thoughtful. "Do all Dantes experience The Inferno? Even your relatives in Florence?"

"My grandfather's cousins are a different branch of the Dante tree. So, their Inferno is experienced differently."

He'd intrigued her. "How does it work with them?"

He drew a shape on her palm. "Instead of the burn you and I share, a mark shows up, a different one for each Dante. When it appears, they know they've touched their soul mate. Since it can take as long as a week for the mark to manifest, they must figure out which of the many women they may have touched is the one meant for them."

"Does the woman also carry a mark?"

Rom frowned. "Eventually, I guess. At least, all the women who have married my Dante cousins bear one. I've asked how it works, but they just laugh and wink. So, I'm not sure what causes the mark to appear, though I could speculate about various possibilities." He smiled. "None of which are appropriate to share with you."

"Mmm. I think I can guess," she retorted dryly.

His smile grew. "To be honest, if I must choose one type of Inferno, I prefer this one since I knew the instant we touched that you were the one."

She had one final question, one that had plagued her from the start. "And how long does The Inferno last?"

"Forever."

"Truly?" She couldn't help the doubt underscoring her question. "Forever?"

He nodded. "One man and one woman for all the years they live. I'm not sure I fully understood, or believed it possible, until I met you. But I understand now. I believe now."

"Do you also believe we'll always feel this way about each other?"

He gave it to her straight. "The Inferno strikes once and only once, Julietta. Dantes have a single soul mate in the whole of the world. Most of the time we are fortunate enough to find her, as I have found you. Sometimes a Dante spends his entire life looking and never discovers the woman meant to be his mate. In that case, he either spends his days alone, or settles for a pale reflection of the real thing."

"Is that what your mother did after your father died?"

He shook his head. "She rarely spoke of The Inferno. She believes it's a curse and claimed it died with my father." She caught the underlying pain sweeping through his words, and her heart went out to him. How horrible to be told the love your parents felt for one another was cursed. "But I always thought she lied in order to protect the life she shares with Luigi. Now that I've experienced The Inferno, I'm even more certain she lied. There's no question in my mind that what I feel for you will last until the end of my days."

Exhaustion settled over her, catching her off guard. "I'm sorry, Rom. Everything is happening so fast. I can't think straight."

He tucked her close. "It's natural to have doubts, especially when what your heart tells you is at odds with what your head is saying."

"Or my family."

"Yes. At some point you'll need to choose between head and heart. Between what your family expects and what is right for you." He cupped her face and tilted it up. "You'll need to choose between me and Tito."

"When you hold me, touch me, the choice is so simple."

He kissed her, his mouth slow and delicious on hers. He didn't rush the embrace. Nor did he deepen it, much to her disappointment. Finally, he released her.

"It isn't the choice that's difficult. It's what happens after you've made that choice. I won't force you, Julietta. It has to be your decision."

Midday the next day, Rom approached the cottage the Bianchi family was using until Julietta's wedding. He could tell the instant Julietta sensed him.

She stood in front of a window box, gently prying a clump of dying roses free from their hard-packed dirt bed. Once again, she wore a simple cotton dress, faded from repeated washings and the bleaching rays of the sun. She'd tied a gardening apron around her trim waist and protected her complexion with the same wide-brimmed straw hat she'd carried when he'd first come across her in the meadow. This time she wore her hair up, the hip-length mass gathered in a heavy knot at the nape of her neck.

At his approach, her back went rigid, and she stilled, as though taking a moment to gather him in and absorb his very essence. "You shouldn't be here," she said without turning around.

He responded with simple honesty. "I couldn't stay away."

She glanced over her shoulder, her reproving frown belied by the amusement in her gaze. "And what will you say if people ask why you're here?"

"I'll tell them the truth," he answered promptly. "Tito told me his fiancée possesses shockingly plump fingers and asked me to resize the engagement ring."

She laughed at his teasing. Then her humor faded—no doubt at the reminder of all that stood between them. In its stead came a pain Rom would have given anything to ease. "The ring's too constricting to wear." She touched a spot beneath the bodice of her dress. "I put it on the chain that holds my crucifix."

The irony of her comment didn't escape him. "That ring will never be the right fit because you and Tito aren't the right fit."

She lifted an eyebrow. "And we are?"

"You already know the answer to that." She frowned at the flowers she'd upended, and he joined her, clicking his tongue in dismay. "You're like these plants, Julietta. If you stay in Santa Lucia, you'll be as choked and root-bound as they are."

"And if I don't stay? Where will we go? After, I mean. Assuming there is an after." She stroked the faded roses with a gloved hand. "Florence?"

He hesitated. He hadn't told her about his job offer or his plan to move to California. He didn't want to panic her. But she deserved to know. Deserved to have all the facts before she made her final decision. "Not Florence."

Her brows pulled together. "But your job is in Florence, isn't it?"

He nodded. "I've been offered a new job. One that will give me the freedom to become a better craftsman. To create my own line of jewelry and receive credit for it."

She swiveled to face him, her expression alight with joy on his behalf. "Rom, that's wonderful. Where's this new job?"

He took a deep breath. "In America. San Francisco, to be precise. That's a city in California."

Her excitement stuttered, fading away, and she stared in disbelief from beneath the wide brim of her straw hat, her eyes dark and shadowed. "Are you serious?"

"Quite serious."

She averted her gaze and returned the small spade she held to her gardening basket. Her hands trembled ever so slightly, and she moistened her lips.

"America," she repeated. "You want me to go with you to America?"

"As my wife, yes."

Julietta stared blindly at the uprooted roses. "I anticipated having to leave home. If I don't marry Tito, I couldn't very well stay. But I thought we'd live in Florence. I . . . I don't know if I can do what you're asking. I don't know if I can leave my family and move so far away."

"We can do it, together."

"Just like that?" she marveled. "Move away from all we've ever known? My roots are here. My family is here. I don't even speak English."

He strove to find the words to convince her. "For some people, it would be impossible. But not for us. We're not like most people from Santa Lucia." He looked around, searching for an analogy. His gaze landed on the nearby grove, and he gestured in that direction. "It's not like we're those orange trees, trapped in a grove."

Despite the underlying seriousness, she shot him a look of amusement. "Then what are we?"

"We're whatever we choose to be. Don't you see, Julietta?" Passion filled his voice. "We're people, people who don't have to follow the dictates of those who would force us to be something we're not."

She slapped the dirt from her gloves and planted her hands on her hips. "How do you know I'm not happy being an orange tree?" she asked in exasperation.

He plucked a pair of shears from her gardening basket. "Do you see those geraniums in the window box over there?"

"I see them."

"Despite the lack of attention, they're flourishing. The rain nourishes them, the sun warms them. They are happy to remain in their box doing whatever it is geraniums are content doing."

"So now we're geraniums?"

"No. *We* are roses." He examined the dying plant she'd removed from the box and shook his head. "Look at the poor thing. The roots are wrapped so tightly around themselves, they can't get sufficient nourishment. Roses don't do well stuck in a box."

She didn't pretend to misunderstand. "And Santa Lucia is our box?"

"Exactly. Being root-bound halts growth and slowly strangles you to death." He ruthlessly clipped the roots in a downward motion, pulling away any that were blackened and dead. Then he massaged the ball, loosening it, before dumping the plant in a bucket of water. "Now it has a chance. Come. Bring your basket."

He grabbed the bucket and a small burlap bag of compost, and headed away from the cottage, toward the field where they'd first met. He paused along the edge of a slope that tumbled gradually toward the meadow, still dotted with a profusion of lilac hyacinths, bright red poppies, and innocent white daisies.

He smiled at her. "What do you think?"

Her gaze lingered on the spot of their kiss. "I think our rose will be happy here," she decided. "I particularly like that it'll mark our first memory of each other."

Rom jiggled the bucket. "What do you say, little rose? Do you approve?"

Julietta laughed. "Did it answer?"

"It did. It says the only thing that might make it happier is if it were within sight of the sea. At least, it would make me happier if I were a rose." His laughter joined hers, the combination creating a sweet harmony. "Okay, to work. What do you say we give this rose a new home?"

Rom dug a hole, while Julietta lined the loosened soil with compost before, together, they planted the rose. After pouring the remaining water from the bucket around the new bed, he turned to Julietta. He pulled her into his arms and kissed her, the memory of their first embrace sweetening the moment. To his relief, she melted against him, still as open and generous as she'd been whenever they'd come together.

"I'm still not sure I'm a rose," she confessed. "But with you, it's what I want to be."

Regret consumed him. "I've asked so much from you in such a short amount of time. And I've done it badly." Gently, he reached beneath the neckline of her dress and eased the silver chain from her neck. He removed the ring and deposited it in his shirt pocket, then returned the necklace to its proper place. Taking her hands in his, he dropped to one knee. "I refuse to propose marriage while you wear another man's ring, even if it's on a chain around your neck."

"Well, technically, it's your ring, too."

He conceded the point. "I suppose it is. Even so, since I'm not the man who put it there, I'd rather you not wear it. At least, not right now."

"I understand."

"Julietta Bianchi, my one and only love, will you marry me?"

Her answer blossomed across her face, as radiant as the sun and as beautiful as the tumble of wildflowers dancing beneath the sun. "Yes, Romero Dante. I'll marry you. I'll even try to become a rose for you."

"I don't want you to be anything other than yourself, which is the perfect woman."

He stood and swept her into his arms, sealing their promise with a kiss. It seemed right to propose here, where it had all started. Just as it seemed right to have freed the root-bound rose bush and planted it as a symbol of what they hoped for the future.

Now all they had to do was figure out how to overcome the small obstacle of a soon-to-be pissed off fiancé and two infuriated families.

What could be easier?

Only a handful of days remained before the wedding—a wedding Julietta knew in her heart would never take place. Not after what happened at the engagement party. And definitely not after Rom's proposal the day before. As determined as she was to marry him, the idea of breaking off her engagement to Tito worried her. But convincing her family she belonged with Rom loomed like an insurmountable obstacle.

"Thank God this marriage is almost behind us," Maria muttered.

Julietta set aside the vegetable brush she'd been wielding, relieved to have the subject raised. Perhaps she could plant a few vital seeds that would persuade her mother to change her mind. With any luck, those seeds would take root and flourish. "If my wedding is causing you so much stress, we can always cancel it," she suggested.

"Cancel? *Per carità!* Don't you dare suggest such a thing," Maria replied with a sharp edge. "Have you any idea—" She turned abruptly away, but not before Julietta caught the telltale glint of tears.

She eyed her mother with concern. Her mother rarely cried. If anything, she was always the calm center in the middle of the family storm. "Mamma? Do I have any idea about what? What's wrong?"

"Nothing." Maria groped for one of the chairs tucked beneath the scarred kitchen table, and sank into it. "Nothing at all."

Julietta hastened to set aside the vegetables she'd washed and joined her mother. "That's not true. There's something you're not telling me.

What is it?" She gathered her mother's work-roughened hands in her own. For an instant, hope filled her. "Does it have to do with my marriage to Tito? Is there some reason I shouldn't marry him?"

"No. No, nothing like that," Maria said, crushing the burgeoning bud of hope. "It's your marriage to Tito that will save us."

"Save us," Julietta repeated. Alarm streaked through her, along with a deepening dread. "Save us from what, Mamma?"

Chapter Six

Maria straightened in her chair. "That's your father's business," she said primly. "And soon, *grazie a Dio*, Tito's."

Julietta fought through her confusion in an attempt to find a logical explanation. "You said my marriage would save us. Is this about the vineyard? Is there something wrong with it?" She frowned. "I thought *Babbo* wanted to sell because the work had become too much for him."

"And so it has." But she refused to meet Julietta's gaze. "Forget I said anything. It will all turn out well once you and Tito are married."

"No, I want the truth. What will turn out well?" she pressed. "Why is it so important for me to marry Tito?"

"It's none of your concern, Julietta," her mother insisted. "Now, let it go."

"You don't understand. I can't let it go. Not now." She took a deep breath, steeling herself for the coming battle. "Mamma, I don't want to marry Tito. In fact, I was going to discuss it with you and *Babbo* later today. We're not suited."

Her mother turned deathly pale, her hand fisting around her crucifix. "You can't back out, Julietta. You mustn't."

"Why?" she demanded. "What's going on?"

She didn't think her mother would answer. Then her face crumpled, and helpless tears slid down her cheeks. "You know we've had a few bad years, all on the heels of the war and all it took from us. There was the frost. Two years ago that horrible drought that shriveled all the grapes. Then last year, the blight took half the harvest."

"But it's looking good for this year, isn't it?"

Maria nodded, though it offered little reassurance. "Unfortunately, your father was forced to borrow money to get us through the winter. The money is due soon. If it's not repaid, we'll lose the vineyard."

Dread pooled in the pit of Julietta's belly. "We don't have the money to repay the loan, do we?"

"No," Maria whispered. "We've done everything possible to keep it quiet, in case Tito caught wind of our problems."

"He doesn't know?"

"No," Maria repeated, her voice sharper this time. "It's important we keep it from him. We need him to marry you."

"So he'll buy the vineyard and the debt can be repaid?" Maria nodded, exhaustion carving deep lines into a face whose beauty had faded before its time. Julietta sat beside her mother in stunned silence. "Why can't you just sell the vineyard, outright? Why must I marry him?" she finally asked.

"Because after our debt is paid, we'll have nothing left. No land. No home. Nothing with which to support eight daughters."

The full ramifications hit Julietta. "If Tito knew we were about to lose the vineyard, he wouldn't need to marry me, would he?"

"No. He could simply wait until we lost the vineyard and buy it for a fraction of its worth."

"Wait." Julietta struggled to absorb the information. "You expect Tito to buy the vineyard and *then* support us? *All* of us?"

"He can well afford it," Maria retorted, stung. She gripped Julietta's arm, her words low and hurried. "It's important you be a good wife to him, Julietta. Your sister was right when she said you must satisfy him in bed. A man will do almost anything for a woman if he's pleased. *A tutti i costi.* No matter what it costs. *Capisci?*"

"It's you who doesn't understand, Mamma," Julietta whispered. "Tito . . . He repulses me."

"You must not let him know." Urgency underscored her mother's words.

"It's too late. He kissed me at our engagement party and—" She broke off, unwilling to go into details. "He knows I didn't enjoy it."

Maria closed her eyes. "We won't force you to marry him. But if you don't, we will be destitute. We'll have to split the family apart, send the little ones to relatives. Are you very sure you can't go through with the marriage? Perhaps in time you won't mind when he—"

Julietta pulled free of her mother's hold and stood. "I'll think about it. It's the best I can do." Unable to help herself, she bolted from the house.

Julietta fled to the meadow and collapsed beside the rose bush she and Rom had replanted. To her amazement, it already showed signs of flourishing.

Unlike her.

She'd never have the opportunity to discover whether she could become a rose and put down roots on a hillside overlooking the sea. Instead, she'd spend the rest of her life root-bound. Tears filled her eyes, and she allowed them to come. Just this once. Just this one time, she'd mourn what would never be. Regret not taking that path with Rom. Because no matter how deeply she loved him, she refused to sacrifice her family for her own happiness.

She felt Rom's approach long before he reached her. She dried her tears, praying he wouldn't notice she'd been crying. A vain hope, no doubt. He took a seat beside her and gathered her hand in his. Showing amazing perception, he didn't say a word but waited patiently for her to speak.

"I have to go through with the wedding," she finally said, her gaze fixed on the distant horizon.

"What happened?" No anger. No resentment. No demands. Just a single, calm question.

She couldn't bring herself to tell him the truth, not when she didn't have the wherewithal to defend her decision should he challenge it. "I realized I'm not a rose."

"Ah."

Why wasn't he fighting her? Why wasn't he arguing? She stumbled into an explanation. "I can't uproot myself and move halfway around the world with a man I've only known for a few days."

"But you can marry a man whose touch repulses you?"

She bowed her head, stung by his gentle inquiry. "Yes."

"Julietta, if you don't wish to marry me, I can accept that. True, I'll do everything within my power to change your mind. But it's your decision. All I ask is for you to wait. Postpone your marriage until you're sure of what you truly want." A quick glance warned he'd set his jaw into a line of endless determination. "I would even be willing to remain in Florence and work for the Dantes, if it meant having you in my life."

She shook her head. "I wouldn't ask that of you."

"You're not. I'm making the offer." He tossed her a tender smile. "Roses flourish in Florence, even ones in boxes. They just need a bit more care."

"I can't."

His eyes narrowed, flaring with hot, gold sparks. "And if I offered to remain in Santa Lucia? To work your father's vineyards in exchange for your hand in marriage?"

Her mouth trembled for an instant before she regained control. "It's a generous offer, Rom. But I'd have to refuse."

"So, you're ending things between us."

"Yes."

"Very well. If there's nothing I can say to change your mind, I must accept your decision."

"I'm sorry. I won't change my mind."

He lifted her hand and kissed the back of it. She fought to keep from shaking. She only needed to remain strong a few more minutes, and it would be over. Rom would express his regret and leave. And she would return to the cottage and continue the preparations for her wedding to Tito. She closed her eyes. How would she bear it?

"One quick question before I leave, *amore mia.*" How could he sound so casual when it felt as though her heart was breaking?

She cleared her throat. "What is it?"

"A few minutes ago, you said you have to go through with the marriage. Why do you *have* to?" Her gaze flashed to his in open alarm, and he smiled. "Ah. I believe that tells me everything I need to know."

She shook her head. "What are you talking about?"

"Why do you have to marry Tito?" he asked again.

"I . . . I never said that."

"Yes, Julietta, you did. It was the first thing you said when I joined you. 'I *have* to go through with the wedding.' Why?"

She came as close to the truth as she dared. "Until you met me, honor was everything to you. Believe it or not, it's important to me, too." She forced herself to continue meeting his gaze, striving to appear resolved. "My family will suffer if I don't marry Tito. How can I be content with you, if they pay the price for my happiness?"

He slipped a hand around her neck and drew her in for a lingering kiss. She returned it with a helpless passion. How would she survive without him? Worse, how could she allow Tito to touch her the way Rom had? She thrust the thought away, unwilling to have anyone else intrude on this final kiss. She closed her eyes, losing herself in his embrace. Their tongues tangled, his breath becoming hers. The heat of The Inferno burned between them, pulsating through her blood and quickening her heartbeat.

"I love you," she moaned against his mouth. "I'll always love you."

"As I will always love you."

She forced herself to pull away and stand. "I beg you, don't attend the wedding. I couldn't bear it."

He bit off a curse and stood, as well. "You couldn't bear it? I know there's something else going on here. Something you're not telling me." His gaze narrowed, grew hard and resolute. "Know this, Julietta. I'll let you go for now. I can't promise to let you go forever."

"Once I'm married to Tito, you'll have to."

"You're not married to him, yet," he retorted. "And if I have anything to say about it, you never will be."

She didn't dare respond. Without another word, she turned and walked away.

Rom continued to sit beside the rose bush for a long time after Julietta left, turning various options over in his mind. Nothing brilliant came to him and, at long last, he stood and brushed the grass from his trousers.

"I always thought Julietta was the weak one," a woman said from somewhere nearby. "But I've underestimated her."

Rom froze, searching the shadows cast by a widespread umbrella pine. After a moment, he found the womanly shape outlined against the tree trunk, her dark brown hair and clothing offering the perfect camouflage. "You, again."

Serena smiled, amusement giving an attractive sparkle to her dark eyes. "Me, again." She stepped into the sunlight. "And, yes, I've been following Julietta—at my mother's request, I might add."

"Do you intend to tell your mother about us?"

Serena tilted her head to one side. "I haven't quite decided."

Rom folded his arms across his chest. "Maybe you should. Maybe we should all sit down and discuss this ridiculous marriage. Get everything into the open."

She gave a short, impatient laugh. "That wouldn't end well for you, I'm afraid."

"I'm willing to take my chances."

She studied him closely, and a curious expression bloomed across her face. "You really love her, don't you?"

Was she kidding? "Of course I love her. What the hell did you think?"

"That you were trying to seduce your best friend's bride."

"That would be dishonorable," Rom said stiffly. Then, realizing the absurdity of his words, he blew out a sigh. "I wish to marry your sister, not seduce her. And though some might find that a somewhat dubious distinction, I consider it an important one."

"Does Julietta feel the same way?" Serena demanded. "She wishes to marry you, too? This isn't some sort of game the two of you are playing?"

"This isn't a game. Your sister also wants to marry me. Or she did, until today. At least,

I thought she did." He frowned, his gaze sharpening. "Do you know what happened to change her mind?"

Serena hesitated, and he could tell she was weighing her options. "Mamma told her if she doesn't marry Tito, we'll be destitute," she admitted candidly. "Even when they marry, what he pays for the vineyard will only relieve my parents of their debt. He'll still end up supporting my entire family."

"Is Tito aware of this?"

He caught a spark of anger in her stance. "No."

Rom shook his head in disgust. "Poor Tito. Of all of us, he's the true victim."

He'd surprised her. "Do you truly believe that?"

He nodded. "I realize you don't hold a high opinion of me. And I understand why. I don't like deception, and yet, that's exactly what I've done. Deceived the people who mean the most to me and Julietta. I would prefer to court your sister openly, to prove my worth and the sincerity of my love for your sister."

"Very noble," she said, a hint of mockery belying her words. "Why don't you do that? I'm sure everyone will be delighted with the match. Tito will gladly relinquish his bride. My parents will be thrilled to welcome you as the perfect son-in-law. And you and Julietta will live happily ever after."

Anger ripped through him. "Then what do you suggest? Do you believe your sister should marry a man whose touch repels her? Sacrifice herself for the benefit of her family? Destroy everyone's lives? Because that's what will happen if she marries Tito."

He caught the flinch Serena couldn't quite suppress at the mention of Tito's name, and intuition created an unexpected connection. "You don't want Tito to marry Julietta, do you?"

"No," she confessed.

He'd found the lever he needed, and he used it ruthlessly. "You realize Tito is the one who will suffer the most," he hammered at her. "All he wants is a damn vineyard. Instead, he's saddled with a responsibility he knows nothing about, and won't know about until it's too late to make an informed choice. And then he'll find himself in a loveless marriage with a wife he'll come to despise and a family he'll need to support. How is that fair?"

"It's not," she agreed. "But there might be a way out, if you're willing."

"Tell me."

"It isn't the most honorable solution," she equivocated.

"I'm still listening."

"I suggest you steal Julietta away right before the wedding ceremony."

For a moment Rom said nothing, then he laughed. Unbelievable. "Just out of curiosity, have you been talking to my grandfather?"

Serena blinked in surprise. "Signore Dante suggested this, as well?"

"Perhaps the three of us should get together."

A smile played at the corners of her mouth. "Maybe we should."

Julietta sat beside her youngest sisters, putting the final stitches in the dresses they'd wear to her wedding. The three of them, ranging from six to ten, were curled up together in bed, sleeping the sleep of the innocent, the soft glow from the bedside light not enough to disturb their slumber.

The past few days had been the most difficult of Julietta's life, the pull of The Inferno a constant ache. Would she always feel the burn, even when Rom lived half a world away? She paused to rub at the itch in her palm. She suspected she would. Maybe, in time, it would bring her comfort, knowing that, once upon a time, she'd known true love, even if only for a moment.

She paused in her sewing to study her sisters. At least by marrying Tito she'd ensure their future. Someday they'd fall in love, too, and her decision would allow them to marry their Romeos instead of more practical suitors. It was worth the sacrifice, she struggled to convince herself. It would have to be, since she'd have precious little else to give her comfort over the coming years.

"Julietta?" Serena stood in the doorway.

Setting aside her sewing, she tiptoed from the room. "What's wrong?"

A flash of compassion slipped across her sister's expression, surprising Julietta. "Nothing's wrong," she said gently. "Mamma would like you to try on your gown so we can make any final adjustments."

"It's fine. I don't need to try it on again."

"Julietta—"

"Please . . ." Her voice broke, and she struggled to control it, to attain the sort of serenity her mother and sister seemed able to adopt with such ease. No doubt she'd have years of practice after her marriage. "Don't ask me to try it on again."

"Is there anything I can do?"

Julietta gathered her composure. "Nothing, *grazie.*" She forced a smile and managed to smooth the rough edges tearing at her words. "Tell Mamma the gown fits beautifully. There will be time before we leave for the church for any final alterations."

"You don't have to go through with this." Serena spoke with uncharacteristic urgency.

"Wouldn't you, if you were in my position?"

"Yes, but—"

"Because you couldn't bear to see your family destitute any more than I can."

Serena started to speak, then closed her mouth. "Julietta, when the time comes, I hope you'll choose the right path."

Julietta closed her eyes, seeing again the dream, the diverging road with the left-hand path leading to Rom. The "right" path, her sister had said. Sadly, that was the one that led to Tito. "I think the right path already chose me."

"Is everything set?" Rom asked.

Nonno inclined his head. "I have spoken to the priest and he has agreed to marry you, even without the banns being read."

Serena frowned. "Does *il sacerdote* realize they'll be eloping?"

"Of course, though he pretends otherwise."

"And he doesn't have a problem with that?"

Nonno shrugged. "He is an old friend. He will look the other way." He patted his various pockets until he found the cigar he'd been searching for and took a moment to light it. A ring of smoke encircled his snowy head, and he stabbed the cigar in Rom's direction. "We won't mention my little lapse to your mamma, no?"

"She'll smell it on you."

He gave a fatalistic shrug. "A bridge to cross when I find it beneath my feet." His brow furrowed in thought, and he clamped the cigar between his teeth, speaking around it. "Now. The *motociclo* is in my gardening shed covered with a tarp. It may be old, but it is trustworthy. If there weren't an ocean or two in the way, you could ride it straight to America."

Rom grinned. "Since I can't, I purchased tickets for our passage to New York, as well as for the train from Florence to Rome."

"They will be looking for you in Florence," *Nonno* warned.

"If they find us, it will be too late. By then, it will be done. Julietta will be my wife in name and in fact. An annulment will not be possible."

"Shall we finalize our plans?" Serena spoke up again. "The walk to the church from the Rossi villa takes forty minutes. We're supposed to leave right at four. When we arrive at the church, Tito will go inside and I'll take Julietta to the prayer garden in order to put the final touches on her dress and hair. Join us there, and you'll have the opportunity you need to whisk her away."

Rom's frown mirrored his grandfather's. "That could prove problematic. What if she fights me? I'm riding a motorcycle. It's not like I can throw her over my lap and ride off with her."

"I guess you'll have to find a way to convince her." She planted her hands on her hips. "Either she loves you and is willing to elope with you, or she isn't. I refuse to sway her. She must choose to go with you."

"And if she has second thoughts, afterward? If she refuses to marry me when we reach the church?"

"Now that, I can help with." Serena held out a thin envelope. "Give her this and all will be well."

Rom eyed it dubiously. "You're sure? It doesn't look like you wrote very much."

"Just three words," Serena said with a laugh. "Trust me. I know my sister. Those three words are all the ones you'll need."

The next few days crept by. And though Rom attempted to visit Julietta, she refused to see him. From the few glimpses he caught of her, she appeared pale and drawn, her attitude one of such sad determination he found it painful to observe.

Tito didn't appear any better. In fact, his friend's expression mirrored his bride's. Were a bunch of grapes truly worth such misery? Rom didn't understand it. But it filled him with a determination of his own, to change the course of all of their fortunes—for the better, even if it wouldn't initially seem that way.

Much to Rom's relief, the morning of the wedding dawned clear and cooler than normal for early June. The entire day assumed a ritualistic feeling. Every action, even one as habitual as his morning shower, was performed with care and attention to detail, knowing he completed each task with Julietta's pleasure in mind.

An hour before the start of the procession, Rom dressed in the suit he'd bought to wear for Tito's marriage, never imagining he'd end up wearing it for his own. He checked his watch and took a deep breath. This was it. It was time.

His mother and stepbrothers were nowhere in sight—no doubt already on their way to the Rossis' villa. But Luigi lingered in the kitchen. He glanced up at Rom's entrance. Without Nicci's presence to temper his attitude, the mask of politeness slipped for an instant, and a wealth of anger and resentment showed through. Then it vanished, and he gestured in the direction of the root cellar.

"Bring up a couple of bottles of wine before you leave. The *Trebbiano*. Your mamma forgot to do it."

Relieved that Luigi didn't plan a confrontation, Rom nodded. "Sure. I'll get them right now."

"Some beer, as well."

Rom opened the heavy wooden door and pulled the chain connected to the overhead light bulb. Steep, narrow steps plummeted downward into a small cellar that stored the produce his mother canned throughout the summer and fall, select bottles of Ranieri wine, and the butter beer *Nonno* put up each year. Halfway down the steps, the door slammed behind him, and he heard the ancient iron key turn in the lock.

"Luigi?" He turned and ran back up the steps. "What are you doing?"

"Making sure you don't disgrace me." Luigi's muffled voice penetrated the thick wood, the sound filled with rage. "Do you think I don't know what goes on under my own roof? *Mi fai schifo*. You disgust me. I know what you have planned, and I won't let you dishonor my family with your disgraceful behavior."

Rom pounded on the door. "You don't understand. Julietta loves me. And I love her."

"You're cursed. Just as your mother was cursed. Once Tito takes the woman for his wife, the curse will end. Make yourself comfortable, *faccia di stronzo*." He seemed to relish the epithet. "This will be your home until tomorrow."

Rom had no idea how long he pounded on the door. He only stopped when his hands, battered and bloody from his repeated attacks on the impervious wood, turned numb. He dropped on to the top step, exhausted.

How long? How long before Julietta became Tito's wife? Half an hour? Or mere minutes from now. Or maybe she'd already spoken her vows. He leaned his head against the door and closed his eyes.

"Julietta," he whispered. "Believe in me. Believe in The Inferno. Don't do it. I beg of you. Don't marry Tito."

Chapter Seven

Julietta stood in front of the mirror while her mother put the finishing touches on her upswept hair. "You look beautiful," Maria said with a sigh.

Her sisters floated around her in a rainbow swirl of pretty gowns. "Beautiful," they all echoed.

Julietta glanced in the small mirror positioned over a simple dresser. She didn't look the least beautiful. She looked tired. And sad. She straightened her shoulders and forced a smile to her lips, not allowing herself to play the part of the martyr. She'd chosen to marry Tito, and she refused to make everyone around her pay for that choice. Not her family. Least of all her soon-to-be husband.

"It's a shame you couldn't wear my wedding dress," Maria fussed.

Julietta shook her head. "Thank you for the offer, but no one wears a black wedding dress anymore, Mamma."

"It had the prettiest white hat to go with it." She tilted her head to one side. "Still, this gown is also pretty, even if it's not traditional."

And it wasn't. In fact, the strapless gown, a gift from her aunt, had initially shocked her mother. The ruched bodice was gathered to one side, accented with crystals and pearls that trailed from breast to hips in a long, fitted line. For the sake of propriety—and much to her mother's relief—it also came with a long-sleeved, bolero jacket that fastened just beneath her breasts, to be worn in church during the ceremony. The satin skirt was covered in several cascading layers of tulle and belled outward at her hips, ending in a modest train that she could manipulate without assistance.

Serena approached and helped with the veil, a waterfall of tulle that matched Julietta's gown, anchoring it to her sister's upswept curls with a handful of pins. "Don't forget, you need to rip the corner for luck before you walk down the aisle."

"I'll remember." Maybe. Not that it mattered. Nothing about this day would bring her luck. If anyone deserved luck, it was the poor bridegroom.

"Come, girls," Maria announced. "We better leave now if we're going to arrive on time."

The procession for the walk to the church gathered in the road just outside the Rossi villa, everyone in their Sunday best, many carrying wildflowers to scatter ahead of the "happy" couple. Tito stood with his family, his expression set in grim and stoic lines. Had there ever been a gloomier bride and groom? Julietta crossed to his side, and he presented her with a bouquet of pungent herbs and orange blossoms, tied with a white ribbon.

"Thank you, it's beautiful."

He offered a strained smile. "Not as beautiful as my bride."

She closed her eyes and sighed. "Oh, Tito," she whispered. "What are we doing?"

"What we must to get what we each want."

She bowed her head. "I'm not sure it's worth it."

"Time will tell."

The street leading to town was lined with well-wishers, and, in keeping with tradition, they put various obstacles in the path of the approaching couple—a broom Julietta needed to pick up to show she'd be a good housekeeper, a crying child to see if the couple would offer comfort and prove themselves good parents. Every step of the way, Julietta wished with all her heart it was Rom at her side, instead of Tito. No doubt Tito wished for a different bride, as well, someone who'd give him the passion she couldn't.

At one point, he lifted her hand and studied her engagement ring. "I see Rom adjusted it."

"Yes. He gave it to my mother last night." She pretended to glance around. "I don't see him. Where is he?"

"His stepfather told me he isn't well. He sent his apologies."

"I see."

Tears filled her eyes, and she forced them back. What did she expect? She'd asked him to stay away, hadn't she? And he'd granted her wish. Besides, how could she possibly say her vows to Tito while Rom watched? Could she do it if their situation was reversed and he was marrying another? No, never!

Eventually, the procession wound its way into Santa Lucia to the front of the church. Tito paused long enough to kiss Julietta's cheek. "I'll see you in a few minutes." For an instant, his gaze lingered on Serena, and then he spun around and disappeared into the cool, dark interior of the vestibule.

Julietta fought to breathe. This was a mistake. A hideous mistake. How could she bear to spend the rest of her life with a man she didn't love? A kind man, but one whose touch repulsed her? She desperately wanted to save her family, to be an obedient and dutiful daughter. But to spend the next fifty years or more trapped in a loveless marriage? To bring children into this world that were a result of such a union?

"Serena, please," she whispered, fighting to draw air into her lungs. "I need to sit for a moment."

Over her sister's shoulder, Julietta could see their mother looking on in concern. Serena waved off the cluster of family members. "Go on in. We have to make a few final adjustments to her hair and gown before the ceremony."

Everyone slowly filtered into the church, and Serena smiled sympathetically, wrapping an arm around Julietta's waist and drawing her toward a shady prayer garden on one side of the church. "It's okay. We're alone. You can relax now."

They crossed to a bench positioned beneath a widespread oak, and Julietta sank on to the wrought-iron seat. "Thank you."

"Would you like some water?"

"Please. And tell Mamma everything will be fine. I'll be along in a few minutes. I just have to catch my breath after the walk into town."

"I'll be right back." Then she did something she'd never done before. She stooped in front of the bench and gathered Julietta close. "Someday I hope this will all come full circle. Until then, know that I love you and only want what's best for you."

She left the garden before Julietta could ask what she meant. But her words lingered, as though they were part of some greater message. In the distance, she heard her father call to one of her younger sisters, and aware her time alone wouldn't last much longer, she closed her eyes. "Rom," she whispered, rubbing the deep, burning itch centered in her palm. "Please, forgive me. I love you. I do. I wish there were another way, but there isn't."

With all her heart, she prayed some alternate solution would present itself in the next few minutes and she'd escape her fate. That a miracle would happen and Rom would ride up and carry her off, and yet her family would still somehow be saved.

But miracles weren't meant for her.

Rom leaned his head against the heavy wooden door and closed his eyes, rubbing the deep, burning itch centered in his palm. He wished with all his heart for a miracle. That somehow he'd be able to escape from the cellar and get to Julietta before time ran out.

As though in answer to his prayer, he heard the key turn in the lock. He leapt to his feet, and the door opened, bright light streaming in and momentarily blinding him. "Romero?"

"Mamma?"

"There isn't much time," she whispered. "Tito and Julietta will be at the church soon, if they're not there already."

"Thank you. Thank you for letting me out."

She cupped his face and kissed him. "I'm sorry, *figlio mio*. When I married Luigi, I thought I was protecting you. Protecting us both. But he's never forgiven me for loving your father."

Rom skimmed his palm with his thumbnail. "It doesn't go away, does it?"

Nicci shook her head. "No. *Che Dio mi perdoni.* May God forgive me, I love your father still. I will always love him, just as you will always love Julietta." Her hands covered his, Dante to Dante, Inferno to Inferno. "But maybe my curse will be your blessing."

"You can come with us."

She shook her head again. "I made my choice a long time ago. My place is here." She stepped aside. "Go. Quickly, Romero. Before Luigi realizes what I've done."

He didn't waste any time. He darted from the house and ran flat out for the garden shed. Just as his grandfather had promised, the motorcycle waited beneath the tarp. It only took an instant to start it. The motor roared to life beneath him, rumbling between his legs. He revved the engine and kicked it into gear.

And then he flew.

Julietta didn't know what distracted her from her revelry. A noise. A low-level hum that grew steadily louder, until it seemed to roar through her veins. She stood and left the small courtyard garden. Only a few stragglers lingered outside the church. Serena was nowhere to be seen, probably in search of the water she'd promised. Julietta glanced toward the doorway leading into the vestibule. Her father hovered there, talking to her sisters. None of them seemed to hear the noise that had captured her attention.

She shaded her eyes and gazed across the piazza, toward the road leading to the Rossis' villa. A plume of dust rose in the distance, rolling rapidly toward her like a turbulent storm cloud. At the center of the angry cloud she saw something black and shiny, shooting toward the town like a bullet. It hit the edges of the piazza, the roar of its engine finally reaching her, and she realized it was a motorcycle.

It barely slowed as it entered the town, hurtling toward the central fountain and around it, pigeons exploding into the air like an advance guard. The rider angled the motorcycle so low into the turn he nearly scraped his shoulder against the dark gray paving stones. Just when she was certain he'd spin out, he righted the machine and flew straight toward her.

It was then she knew.

Her prayers had been answered.

Her miracle had arrived.

Rom skidded to a stop, directly in front of Julietta. "Come with me," he called over the roar of the motorcycle.

He saw the yearning in her gaze, as well as the hesitation. He held out his hand. It was bruised and bloodied, crusted with dirt. She stared at it in shock, tears filling her eyes. She said his name, although the sound didn't reach him over the engine noise. In the midst of all the chaos, time suddenly slowed, just as it had the moment he'd first seen her.

The late afternoon sunshine slanted between the cluster of buildings, casting a soft, golden glaze on their surroundings. In the distance, he sensed sound and movement all around them. A man running from the doorway of the church. People in the square pointing and shouting. A flock of pigeons circling chaotically around the fountain. But in the nexus of it all, he and Julietta were alone, in a world apart.

Everything around him faded to sepia, and all he saw was the woman he loved. Her glorious hazel eyes glittered with brilliant green highlights, and a rosy flush of pleasure bloomed across the high sweep of aristocratic cheekbones. Her sweet mouth slowly curved into a smile, and words trembled on her lips.

"Thank you."

Even so, she made no move to join him. In that instant, he understood she was thanking him for loving her, not thanking him for rescuing her. He continued to offer his hand, their entire future teetering in the balance. Then the oddest thing happened.

He suddenly saw two versions of himself, one on each of a pair of diverging roads. On the shadow-darkened right-hand path he traveled alone, achieving accolades and acclaim, but never having anyone to share his success with. On the left path, Julietta walked at his side along a road lined with heavily laden fruit trees. There were dark spots along the way, but most of the path contained sunshine, the journey bright and colorful and crowded with others, their faces and shapes not quite in focus, as though they were a promise awaiting fulfillment.

"Trust me," he called to her. And still she hesitated. Forever afterward, he never knew where the words came from, whether borne of desperation or love or instinct. Maybe all of those things. Or perhaps The Inferno guided him, whispering the only words that would get through to her. He lifted his voice to a demanding shout. "Take the left path, Julietta!"

She stared in disbelief, and the bouquet of herbs she clutched tumbled to her feet. She held out a hand, one that still bore the ring he'd designed for Tito. It trembled for an instant, a panicked glitter of diamonds and sapphires, then became rock-steady. Her hand linked with his, Inferno melding with Inferno, and time jolted into motion once again. He pulled the ring from her finger with one hand, and with the other swept her on to the motorcycle behind him.

"Hold on tight," he called over his shoulder.

He spun the bike in a swift circle and flipped the ring in the direction of the man running toward them—Julietta's father, if Rom didn't miss his guess. And then he gunned the engine. The back tire skidded on the paving stones before catching, and he shot back across the piazza toward the road leading to Florence.

What had she done? What had she done? *What had she done?*

Julietta buried her face against Rom's broad back, fighting the panic that threatened to overwhelm her. By choosing love, she'd just ruined her family. How could she possibly live with the guilt? How could she create a successful future with Rom when it would always be tainted by the price her family had paid for her happiness?

She had no idea how long they rode. It seemed like hours before they reached a fork in the road. A sign pointed toward Florence to the right. No doubt he intended to take her to his Dante relatives. Maybe they'd talk some common sense into Rom. Maybe they'd help straighten out this mess. Her arms tightened around Rom. Or maybe they'd offer words of wisdom that would allow her to pretend that what she'd done would work out.

To her surprise, he flew past the turn toward Florence. Her veil ripped away at the juncture, floating high in the air before settling on the signpost and her hair loosened. It tumbled free about her shoulders, flying behind her like a flag of freedom. Julietta couldn't help herself. She laughed, even though there really wasn't anything the least bit funny about the situation. A ripped wedding veil was supposed to be lucky. Was it also lucky to have her veil ripped completely away? Or a figurative signpost pointing toward disaster?

Rom continued farther down the road, turning on to a small, narrow lane to their left. He slowed to avoid an obstacle course of ruts and stones. A short time later he idled to a stop outside of a small church. It had seen better days, but someone had made an effort to decorate for a wedding. Flower petals created a path to the doorway of the vestibule, and pretty bows hung above the threshold. *Nonno* sat on the steps waiting for them.

"I'd begun to worry," he said, slowly standing. He eyed his grandson's hands and raised an eyebrow.

"Small delay," Rom replied briefly. "Nothing to worry about."

"If you say so." *Nonno* gave a fatalistic shrug. "The important thing is you're here."

Rom helped Julietta off the motorcycle and swept her into his arms, kissing her with a passion that left her breathless, her guilt vying with a shattering joy. "I don't suppose there's someplace we can freshen up before the ceremony?" he asked his grandfather. He continued to hold her in a close embrace, as though unwilling to break contact with her ever again. "We're a little the worse for wear."

Julietta touched his arm. "Rom . . ."

He glanced down at her and smiled sympathetically. "You're having second thoughts." It wasn't a question.

"And third and fourth," she confessed. "It's not because of you."

He nodded in perfect understanding. "It's because of your parents and their debt."

She stared in shock. "You know about that?"

He released her with notable reluctance. "Serena told me." He patted his trouser pockets and removed a crumpled envelope. "She also asked me to give this to you. It's supposed to explain everything, to reassure you somehow, though I'm not certain how that's possible considering she wrote only three words."

Julietta accepted the envelope and turned it over, carefully unsealing it. Inside she found a single piece of paper, and as Rom warned, three brief words scrawled in her sister's handwriting. She closed her eyes, tears pressing for release.

"What does it say?" Rom asked.

Nonno nodded. "I must admit. I am curious about this, too."

Julietta fought for control. "It says, *I love him.*"

It took a moment for Rom to make the connection. "Tito? She loves *Tito?*" His amazement faded, and certain key puzzle pieces clicked into place. "I guess it makes as much sense as anything we've experienced over the past few days. Perhaps she's hoping to become his bride in your place."

"Knowing Serena, she'll handle the situation quite differently."

Rom gathered Julietta's hands in his. "Does this help, *amata mia?* Can you enter into our marriage without guilt weighting your heart?"

She drew in a deep breath. "I suspect we'll always experience a certain amount of guilt. It's only natural."

He nodded, lifting her hands and kissing them. "We've hurt our families, even if everything works out for them in the end. We weren't able to fall in love and marry in as honorable a way as we would have chosen." Regret tarnished his gaze. "Unfortunately, we weren't given much choice. There was no way to convince your family I would make you an acceptable husband."

"Just as there was no way to convince your family that The Inferno is a blessing." She fought to come to terms with a decision she could no longer change and which she wished had never been forced upon her. "We did the best we could, and now we live with the consequences of our actions, for better or worse."

Rom grinned. "I've seen the consequences. I think they'll mostly be for the better."

His words came back to her, the words that had ultimately convinced her to take his hand and make a leap of faith. "I thought I was the one with the 'eye.' How did you know about the left-hand road?"

He shook his head, his amusement fading. "It just appeared in front of me. Two roads, one leading to a life of joy and abundance—"

"—the other to loneliness," she finished for him. "I saw it, too."

"Then you know we've chosen the right road. Are you ready, my love?" he asked tenderly. "Are you willing to take the first step toward joy?"

She wrapped her arms around his neck and lifted her face to his. "We've already taken the first step. Now we take all the steps that come after."

Tito sat on a wrought-iron bench in the prayer garden alongside the church, relieved everyone had finally taken their pity and left him in peace. He stared moodily at the stone statues placed at strategic points along the various pathways. No doubt they were meant to inspire calm and serenity. They weren't working.

He'd never seen it coming. Never for a moment believed his best friend would steal away his bride. Well, Rom was welcome to her. *May he find joy in her cold arms and their even colder marital bed.*

The clanking of a nearby gate captured his attention, and he glanced up to see Serena enter the garden. Anger shot through him. Great. Just what he needed. Another Bianchi woman. Just perfect. "Are you here to apologize for Julietta?" he demanded at her approach. "For your family?"

For some reason, she didn't look the least apologetic. Instead, she confronted him with a lifted eyebrow. "Apologize for what?" she had the nerve to ask. "In my opinion, you had a lucky escape. You should be grateful my sister left you for Romero, not angry."

"Then why are you here, if not to beg my pardon?" He glared at her. "Perhaps your parents think I'd accept you in place of Julietta. Is that why you're here, as some poor substitute?"

Her anger rose to meet his. "First, I'm no one's substitute. Any man would be lucky to have me, Tito Rossi. Even you. *Especially* you. And second, you can't have me that easily."

What the hell? "Who said I want you?"

She eyed him boldly. "I say. You've wanted me from the start, just as I've wanted you. Deny it, and I'll know I've given my heart to a liar."

She'd shocked him and he slowly stood. "Your heart?"

She tossed back her hair, long, straight hair as inky as the nighttime sky and as different from her sister's as midnight from midday. "Do you think I'm an easy woman?" she demanded, her gypsy-dark eyes flashing with disdain. "That I'd kiss my sister's fiancé just for fun? That I'd risk hurting her, unless I had strong feelings for the man involved? That I'd go against my parents' plans for me on a whim?"

Memories of their kiss crowded in, rushing though him in a molten stream. She'd tasted so sweet, so earthy and ripe. And they'd fit together as perfectly as he and Julietta had fit together imperfectly. He also remembered his parting words to her, "It should have been you." He'd been more right than he'd realized. "Are you saying you love me?" he asked abruptly.

"I do if you're the man I believe you to be," she stunned him by replying. "Shall we find out?"

"How?"

She closed the distance between them, stopping him when he'd have taken her into his arms. "First, we need honesty between us."

He thrust a hand through his hair and eyed her grimly. "It would make for a pleasant change."

"I agree. And part of that honesty means telling you that I encouraged my sister to run away with Rom. That I helped her, though my parents knew nothing about it."

Anger ripped through him. "Why would you do that?"

She vacillated, clearly hesitant to confess the full extent of her crimes, despite her desire for honesty. "I wish I could say I did it for altruistic reasons, that Julietta's happiness meant more to me than any other consideration."

"But that would be a lie." He was learning to read her.

She bowed her head. "Yes. I didn't want her to marry you. Not after what happened between us the night of your engagement party. You were wrong for each other. But we—" She looked at him, and her heart crept into her gaze. "We were right. So very right."

He couldn't deny it. "And now you expect me to marry you in her place?"

To his surprise, Serena shook her head. "No. Not until we're certain it's what we both want. And not until my parents agree that I'm not meant for the convent and my sister Rosa should take my place."

"What about the vineyard?"

She took a deep breath. "I need to tell you something, something that will change everything between us."

Suspicion filled him. "Go on."

"My parents borrowed money against the vineyards. That money comes due soon. If they can't pay it, we'll lose our home, and you'll be able to purchase the vineyard for far less than what my parents are asking—and without having to marry in order to own it."

"What?"

She faced him, her shoulders squared, her rounded chin set at a combative angle. For some peculiar reason, it made her even more appealing. A rebellious hen defying the cocky rooster. "We'll lose everything. We'll be destitute. But you'll own your precious vineyards."

He should have been happy with the news. Why wasn't he happy? Why wasn't he shoving past her and celebrating his narrow escape? Instead, he found himself rooted in place.

"Or?" he found himself prompting.

She took a deep breath. "Or you can court me. Properly. Though not with the ring meant for my sister. Allow me some pride. Once you're certain I'll make you a suitable wife—and I will—

you can pay off my parents' debt." Her mouth curved into a wry smile. "No doubt you'll pay far more than that since my parents will have nothing but a rich son-in-law to provide for them and my sisters."

"And why would I do that?"

She continued to face him without flinching. "Because you'll also have me. It's your choice whether you have just the vineyards, or if you have a family who will adore you and a wife who will love you like no one else will ever love you." She gripped her hands together, and he suddenly realized they were shaking. She was shaking. He could understand it. She was risking everything with her confession. "I'm telling you all of this because I won't go into a marriage with any deception between us. When you make your choice, it will be with all the facts."

And now the decision was his. Two roads opened before him, as sharp and clear as a summer's day. The left-hand road offered glittering success and wealth, following in his father's footsteps. The right-hand road also offered success, but of a different sort. This road held more trials and tribulations, his success hard-won and long-fought. But on that road stood Serena, beautiful and passionate, along with a son and daughter. And while his daughter stood in shadow, Rom's ring on her finger, his son stood in brilliant sunshine, his eyes as dark and brilliant as his mother's. Tito knew which road he wanted.

And he took it.

He hooked a finger in the neckline of Serena's blouse and gave a gentle tug. She stepped into his arms, the fit as perfect as the first time they'd embraced. "You put a high price on yourself."

"Yes, I do." She lifted her mouth to his. "But I'm worth it."

She proved it with a slow, thorough kiss that made promises he couldn't wait for her to fulfill. They didn't speak for a long time. When they parted, both a bit more rumpled and a lot more breathless, it was Serena who, in typical fashion, cut right to the heart of the matter.

"What about Rom and Julietta? Do you think you can forgive them?"

He nodded. "I forgave them as soon as I realized I'd been saved from a cold, miserable marriage."

"Can you convince my parents not to chase after them?"

"I'll do what I can."

She sighed in relief. "When are you going to tell Rom and Julietta that all is forgiven?"

He frowned, anger still grumbling beneath the surface. "You assume a lot. I don't recall saying all is forgiven."

She smiled knowingly. "When?"

Tito shrugged. "Eventually." Then he grinned. "But not until they've had a few years to wallow in their guilt and suffer for what they did. After all, they've saddled me with an irritating wife who will nag me incessantly."

"Probably."

He released a reluctant sigh. "But at least you'll warm my bed."

"Such a tepid description. Don't you long for something far more than mere warmth?" She caught his earlobe between her teeth and gave him a gentle love bite. "Maybe something as hot as Mt. Vesuvius."

He shuddered. "You would have made a lousy nun."

"So I keep telling everyone." She wrapped her arms around Tito's neck. "But I'll make a superb wife."

Chapter Eight

Julietta didn't remember much of the wedding ceremony, only dreamy moments awash with soft color and sound. *Nonno's* gruff laugh when he tucked a bit of iron in Rom's pocket to ward off evil spirits. His gifting her with his handkerchief to cover her loosened hair, to use in place of the veil she'd lost. His ripping a corner for luck. The shadowy coolness inside the sanctuary. The dust motes that danced in the dying rays of sunlight filtering through the latticework of the confessional. Her confession and the balm of forgiveness. The purifying scent of incense and the ritual of the Mass. The sanctity of their ultimate joining. The kindness in the voice and gaze of the elderly priest when he blessed their union. The weight of the handcrafted gold band Rom slid on her finger. The kiss of her husband, the first as his wife. The passion that lingered like a promise behind that kiss.

The impressions all melded together into a delicious medley of scents and sounds, tastes and touches. But the image that remained first and foremost was the sheer adoration and love on Rom's face when they were pronounced husband and wife. His eyes blazed molten gold with the intensity of his feelings for her, feelings she returned with every particle of her being.

They exited the church into twilight. A photographer waited for them, another gift from *Nonno*. Julietta and Rom faced the camera nervously and Rom took Julietta's hand, squeezing it tight. They glanced at each other an instant before the photo was snapped, and relaxed into the certainty of their love. The photographer grinned in delight at capturing the candid moment and promised to have a copy ready for them the next morning.

Nonno stepped forward and kissed the bride. *"Evviva gli sposi,"* he said, offering the traditional post-ceremonial greeting. Tears gathered in his eyes as he pulled his grandson in for a warm hug. "It hurts my heart to say farewell, even as it fills me with joy to see your happiness. Know I go with you in spirit, *nipote.*"

Rom thumped his grandfather on the back and reluctantly released him. "The invitation is still open, *Nonno*. You're welcome to join us, anytime."

"Who knows what God has in store for us? Perhaps there will be occasion for a visit." He released his breath in a heavy sigh. "In a few minutes I must go and visit some old friends so

I have a story to cover my actions. When I return to Santa Lucia and hear of your disgrace, I will show great sadness over my wayward grandson. And of course, I will know nothing of how such a thing might have happened."

Rom eyed his grandfather grimly. "Don't take any *merda* from Luigi."

Nonno chuckled. "He will not dare, considering I contribute heavily to the support of his family." He removed a thick envelope from his jacket pocket. "This is for you and your lovely bride. For emergencies."

Rom shook his head and held up his hands. *"Nonno,* I don't need your money."

But his grandfather wouldn't be denied and forcibly tucked the envelope in his grandson's pocket. "It is mine to give as I see fit. It is my legacy to you, along with this." He handed over a small box. "Consider it a *bon voyage* present. Then, tomorrow, Aldo will come to take you to Florence. That will be my last gift to you."

"Thank you," Julietta said and embraced Rom's grandfather. "Thank you for everything."

An ancient car pulled up and honked. "That is my ride." Tears fell to *Nonno's* cheeks, sliding into the heavy crevices lining his face. He wiped the dampness away with shaky hands. "I seem to have lost my handkerchief," he joked gruffly.

Julietta removed the scrap of linen he'd given her to use for a veil and gently dried his tears before kissing each cheek and then his mouth. *"Sarai sempre nel mio cuore,"* she whispered. "You will always be in my heart."

And then he was gone, leaving the newlyweds with the bitterness of parting, combined with the sweetness of loving memories.

"Where do we go now?" Julietta asked afterward.

"Nonno arranged for a small cottage for our wedding night. It's not far from here."

"But I don't have anything to change into." He grinned, and she nudged him with her hip, pretending exasperation. "And in the morning? What do you expect me to wear then?"

His grin widened. "The same as what you'll wear tonight." He lifted her into his arms and swung her in a dizzying circle. "Calm yourself, wife. Your sister has seen to all your needs. She even arranged to have the bulk of your clothing sent to Florence. I'm not sure how she managed all she did, but I've concluded your sister is a force of nature. I don't think Tito has any idea what's about to hit him."

Julietta clung to Rom's neck, laughing. "Should I warn that it runs in the family?"

"What man wouldn't want a capable woman at his side? Be a force of nature, *amore mia*. I don't fear it. I welcome it."

Her laughter faded. "I hope we'll always feel this way about each other."

"You have doubts?"

She shrugged. "It's just that we haven't known each other very long. What happens if we irritate one another?"

"The road here had many rocks and ruts. But we maneuvered around them. We'll continue to maneuver around them. Together."

"And if we trip or fall?"

"I will help you stand again, just as you will help me." He leaned in and kissed her, his strength becoming her strength. "We will dust each other off and kiss our hurts and bruises. Then we'll continue down the road, hand in hand. We will love together, have children together, build a life together. And we'll grow old together. You know it's true. You've seen it, just as I have."

She couldn't deny it. "It won't be a perfect life."

"It never is." His tone grew serious. "But it will be perfect for us."

Night fell just as they reached the cottage they'd been offered for their wedding night. It belonged to an elderly couple who were visiting relatives in Rome. Someone had left a cold dinner for them in the refrigerator—a cheese and olive plate, roasted chicken, several pasta dishes, and a small wedding cake—though neither of them were hungry. At least, not for food.

Nonno had added one more surprise. In the middle of the floor was a vase, decorative plastic pearls glued to it and their names painted around the base. Julietta laughed. "Is he serious?"

"Knowing my grandfather, very. He's a man who holds his traditions dear."

"So, we should smash it?"

"Of course. We can count the pieces while we pick up the fragments." He frowned in mock seriousness. "How else will we know how many years our marriage will last? Come, we'll do it together."

Between them, they hoisted the vase above their heads and smashed it down on to the stone floor of the kitchen.

"Per cent'anni!" Rom exclaimed. For a hundred years.

And sure enough, when they swept the last clay shard into the rubbish bin, it added up to a magical one hundred. "Do you suppose we could be so lucky?" Julietta marveled from her position on the floor.

"With you, I think anything is possible."

She smiled at him over her shoulder, then stilled, taking a moment to simply drink him in, absorbing him into her skin and feeling the rush of his essence heat her blood and kick her heartbeat into a swift rhythm of rising passion. She'd wondered what it would be like to give herself to this man, physically, as well as emotionally. That time had come, and the nervousness and fear of the unknown faded away like dew beneath the warming balm of the sun.

She remained seated on the floor, the skirt of her dress billowing around her. Slowly she removed the bolero jacket and set it aside. Then she swept her hair off her back, silently presenting him with the row of tiny buttons that punctuated the length of her spine. After the slightest hesitation, he crouched behind her. His heat surrounded her, warmed and aroused her. She marked the progress of his hands by the slow give of her gown, each button gently released until the fitted bodice fell away.

Julietta sighed. How she wished she wore delicate silk and lace beneath her gown. But finances hadn't allowed for anything so luxurious. Her strapless bra was a simple white cotton, decorated with a small blue bow, added to satisfy part of the wedding custom "something old, something new, something borrowed, something blue." The plain cotton matched the equally plain high-waisted panties hidden by her petticoats.

Rom unhooked the back strap, and she allowed the bra to fall away. She turned in place, and he simply stared, shaking his head. "You look like Aphrodite, with the sea foaming around you," he said, his voice low and husky.

"I'm not a goddess. I'm just a woman."

"Fortunate, since I'm just a man."

"My man."

He lifted her from the floor, freeing her from her gown and petticoats. "And my woman."

She still wore her garter and stockings, along with the despised cotton panties. Not that he seemed to mind. He cupped her face and pulled her in for a slow, tender kiss, one she returned with all her heart. He lifted her into his arms and carried her through to the section of the cottage set aside for the bedroom. It wasn't a separate room, just a generous space off the main area, tucked behind a filmy curtain of gauze.

He set her on the bed, the mattress so wide and soft, it threatened to swallow her. She couldn't help laughing at the way she sank into its depths. Rom followed her down, frowning in dismay. "How am I supposed to be romantic and sophisticated when I'm floundering like an elephant caught in a quagmire?"

"I think the more urgent question is how you're going to explain the loss of your wife," she teased. "'I'm sorry Signore and Signora Bianchi. The last I saw of her, she was vanishing down the gullet of a down mattress.'"

For an instant her joke fell flat, the realization striking them both that there wouldn't be any future conversations with her parents or family. Nor with his.

He closed his eyes and sighed. "I'm sorry, Julietta. I'm sorry loving me meant losing them."

She caught his face between her hands, forcing him to look at her. "We're not going to spend our life pretending they never existed. We're not going to avoid mentioning them because we're afraid we'll cause each other pain. They're part of us and will be part of our children and our children's children. So, right here and now, we make an agreement. We *will* talk about them. We'll celebrate the time we had with them. We'll regret that, for the moment—and only for the moment—they can't share in our joy. But we will pray that one day in the near future, we will be reunited with them. And then our happiness will become theirs."

He took her hands in his and kissed them. "I've married a wise woman. You're right. This can either remain a shadow between us, or we can drag it out into the sunshine and not allow it to grow into a monster lurking in the dark."

She linked her arms around his neck. "And now, husband. Please unearth me from this hungry bed and make mad, passionate love to me. This is one part of my wifely duties I'd like to learn." She offered a siren's smile. "And learn well."

Rom didn't require any further prompting. He suspected his wife hid her nervousness beneath bold words and a tantalizing smile. If truth be told, he had a few nerves, as well, desperately wanting the night to be perfect—especially since so much of their romance had been the opposite.

He left the bed long enough to remove his clothing, taking his time so she could see and accustom herself to the man she'd married. Nude, he returned to the bed and sat beside her. God had gifted her with an endless bounty of hair, the rich, brown curls the most glorious he'd ever seen gracing a woman. They framed her delicate features and slender torso like a vibrant halo of bronze. He helped her strip away her few remaining undergarments, noting the faint blush that spoke of her unease at being completely naked in his presence. He didn't touch her, which he knew surprised her.

"There's no rush." He offered the explanation with an easy smile. "Let's become comfortable with each other first. We will look until we are no longer self-conscious. Then we will touch until we know each other better than we know ourselves. And finally, *adorata mia,* we will make love. And it will be exactly right, the most natural thing in the world."

Her gaze darted like a hummingbird moth, stroking him with its velvety wings. A blush continued to tint her face, and he kept their conversation light and casual until her color returned to normal and she replied to his questions without any lingering awkwardness. Keeping his movements slow and casual, he came down beside her and slid his arm beneath her shoulders, scooping her against his side. Her heart skittered nervously and her breathing quickened. Again, he gave her time to relax, asking about her sisters and teasing her for being called the "easy" one.

"I suspect you've worked hard to keep your true nature hidden."

She turned her head to look at him, her hazel eyes alight with laughter. "Are you saying you don't think I'm easygoing?"

He tapped the end of her nose with his index finger. "I think you're warm and compassionate. I know for a fact you're dutiful and put your family before yourself."

"Until today," she whispered.

"There's a difference between being dutiful and loving your family, and sacrificing yourself," he replied. "If we have a daughter, would you ask such a thing of her?"

"Never." Her response came without thought, passion vibrating through that single word. She released a slow sigh. "No. I'd never ask a child of mine for so great a sacrifice."

"Just as your parents should never have asked it of you."

It was as though he'd lifted a great weight from her shoulders. Tears welled in her eyes, and she curled into him. "They shouldn't have insisted I marry Tito, should they?"

"I'm sure they wouldn't have, if they hadn't thought it would be in your best interest, as well as their own."

"Do you think Serena and Tito will marry?"

He laughed, though it sounded more sardonic than amused. "Probably." He kissed the top of her head and her curls clung to the hint of shadow roughening his jaw. "The only question is whether Tito is willing to go through with another wedding."

"You mean it depends on whether he loves Serena as much as she loves him."

Unable to help himself, he stroked his wife's bare shoulder, lingering on the fragile sweep of her collarbone. Her skin flowed like silk beneath his hands. "Or whether his desire for your family's vineyard outweighs the dent his ego took today."

She froze beneath his touch, and he reluctantly stilled his roving hand. "No," she whispered. "Don't stop."

"Are you sure?"

"Very sure."

He lowered his head and kissed her, taking her mouth in a slow, deep kiss. She responded instantly, her lips parting, her tongue tangling with his. Her breath shuddered from her lungs, and for the first time, she touched him in return. Her hands shifted across his chest, exploring the hard, masculine angles. She murmured against his mouth, something that sounded like approval. And then her hands slid lower, arrowing along the pathway of crisp hair to his erection.

Her touch grew tentative, and he released a sound that hovered between gruff laughter and a groan. "You won't hurt me," he told her. "Though you might unman me."

"You feel strange."

"You'll become accustomed to the strangeness."

"I never realized men were such an interesting combination of soft and hard."

He shot her a speaking look. "With luck, the hard will prevail."

Her laughter bubbled free. "That's not what I meant."

"I'm relieved to hear it."

"I meant—oh, never mind."

He cupped her breasts and kissed them, one after another, watching the nipples tighten into rosy pearls. "You meant you thought all parts of a man were rough and abrasive."

"Yes." The word escaped on a gasp.

"Whereas I find every part of you soft. Soft and warm and sweet."

It was his turn to drift downward. He trailed his fingers from the soft to the warm to the sweet he'd mentioned—across her soft abdomen to the warmth gathering between her legs, and inward to the sweet honey that would ease his passage when he took her virginity. She opened to him, no longer ill at ease with their nudity. But then, from the moment they'd first touched, she'd belonged to him, just as he belonged to her. Despite the conflict sparked by The Inferno, the inability to deny or turn from it, it graced them with love, removing all resistance and bringing endless joy and passion to their union.

Even so, he refused to rush the moment, intent on giving his wife the most pleasure possible. He caught her nipples between his teeth and gently bit down. Her breath hissed from her lungs, and she forked her fingers into his hair, pulling him tight against her breasts.

"Easy, *amore,*" he murmured.

He continued to stroke her thighs, feeling the delicious shivers his touch aroused. He threaded his hand through the thick pelt of curls between her legs. They were unbelievably silky, and he tugged tenderly before sliding a finger inward, deep into liquid heat. Her muscles contracted around him, and she moaned. It was such a delicate, feminine sound, as delicate and feminine as the woman he held in his arms. He slowly withdrew his finger and teased the small nub at the top of her cleft. She cried out, shuddering against him.

More than anything he wanted to mate his body to hers. But he clung to his control. There was still pleasure to share and an entire night in which to share it. He kissed a path downward, pausing to nibble at the soft hollow of her abdomen. Her belly quivered, and the tiniest giggle burst through her moan. He could only hope their lovemaking always contained both laughter and lust. And right then and there, he made himself a promise to make that a priority in their lives. After all, what could be better?

He slid farther downward, inhaling the fragrant essence of her, kissing the silken curve of her thighs. She stiffened ever so slightly, and he calmed her nervousness with a steadying hand. "There's nothing to fear."

"I'm not afraid. I'm . . ." Her head moved restlessly on the pillow.

"Look at me, Julietta." She struggled to focus on him. "You're what?" he prompted.

"Madly in love with you."

It was all he needed to hear. He kissed the very heart of her, stoking the liquid fire to an incandescent inferno. She cried out again, and the muscles in her thighs and belly rippled convulsively, warning of her impending climax. She lifted her hips, and he shifted upward, fitting his body to hers. Slowly, he eased inward, sheathing himself in her heat, stoking it to a white-hot flame. She clenched around him, a low keening moan escaping her throat.

"I'm hurting you," he said through gritted teeth. "I'm sorry. I wanted to make this moment perfect."

"You're not hurting me. And making love to my husband *is* perfect."

Her legs slid around his waist, and she clung to him, matching his movements with an awkward hesitation which gradually gave way to the perfect dance of love. He'd never seen anything more exquisite than the joy blooming across her face as she found her rhythm, discovering the burgeoning seeds of her feminine power.

Watching that transition humbled him, excited him, drove him to give her every pleasure. He could actually see the approach of her climax. Her eyes turned a luminous green, and a rosy flush mounted her cheeks and spread across her chest. Her breath grew short, and she made the sweetest sound, a song all her own, a mating call meant for him and him alone.

And then she convulsed around him, her orgasm shredding the last of his self-control. He drove home, losing himself in her heat, slamming into his own release and tumbling with her over the edge. They clung to each other for endless moments afterward, struggling to find air enough to breathe and wit enough to speak.

"I love you," he whispered against her mouth.

"Always and again," she answered.

He lifted an eyebrow. "Again?"

She smiled, no longer a budding girl, but a woman in full bloom. "Oh, yes. Again and still again until the end of time."

"May we live forever." He grinned. "Assuming, of course, I survive the night."

With the first rays of morning pinking the sky, Rom and Julietta woke, ravenous, both for food and for each other. After satisfying both appetites, they collapsed on the bed, damp and sated, reveling in their first day as husband and wife.

He kissed a path from mouth to breast and back again. "You are beautiful, *amore mia*. The most beautiful woman I have ever known."

She fixed him with a serious gaze. "I can't say you're beautiful in return. Not if I'm honest."

He shrugged. "I know I'm not. You aren't hurting my feelings by saying what my mirror tells me each morning."

She cupped his face. "Oh, hush. What use is a beautiful man? There's something about you far more compelling than beauty. A strength of character. A nobility of spirit. It makes other men seem colorless and boring. You are my Primo. My first love. My only love. It's a name that suits you, somehow. In fact . . ." She tilted her head to one side, her gaze taking on a distant look he was coming to recognize. "I think that's what I'll call you from now on."

"Primo Dante." He tested the shape and texture of the name and nodded. "I like it. It will be a new name to start a new life."

He took her hand in his, The Inferno flaring between them. "I wish to show you something." He eased the thick gold wedding bands from both their fingers and handed her the set. "I made these for us."

She smiled tenderly. "I'll always appreciate the ring you designed for Tito on my behalf, even though it wasn't meant for me."

"No, it wasn't." He gestured toward the bands. "But these are."

"Which is why I adore them." She held them tight within her hand, The Inferno infusing them with the strength of her love for her husband. "Why they will always mean the world to me."

"Look inside," he prompted. "They're inscribed."

She turned his band into the light and read the poetic script. *"Chosen by flame."*

"And now yours."

"Through love decided."

"The Inferno chose us, *bellezza*. But it was your love that has brought us to this place. Your decision to trust in that love." He turned the ring over to show her the tiny design he'd etched into the surface, the same design on each ring. "Every year of our marriage I will add to the pattern, though it will never be completed."

Her brows pulled together. "Why not?"

He gave a fatalistic shrug. "When we depart this world, parts of our life remain incomplete. There are always threads that linger after we're gone." He returned the band to her finger. "So it will be with our rings."

Her frown vanished, replaced by understanding. "Just as life alters us year by year, you'll alter our rings. They'll constantly change and grow, just as we'll constantly change and grow." Her smile held an infinite amount of love. "But it will always be together, a matched set."

He kissed her, delighting in the ease with which she opened herself to him, her desire flaring at his slightest caress. "Yes, *amore*. Together forever."

They made love again, welcoming the day with passionate abandon. Afterward, they raced for the shower, scrubbing each other clean, only to tumble into bed once again. It wasn't until much later that Julietta shot upright.

"I just remembered." She scrambled off the mattress. *"Nonno's* present. Let's see what he gave us."

Rom smiled indulgently at her feminine enthusiasm. She carried the box to the bed and carefully placed it in the middle. He removed the paper wrapping to reveal an enameled

Day Leclaire

wooden chest. Unable to restrain herself, Julietta opened the lid. Inside were endless packets, carefully inscribed in his grandfather's handwriting.

"What are they?" she asked, clearly confused.

It took him a moment to speak. "Seeds." He lifted a packet to show her. "Seeds from his garden."

"To transplant in our new home." She caught her breath in delight. "Oh, Primo. It will be like having a piece of his heart along with us."

She understood so clearly, attuned to him like no one else he'd ever known. He nodded, gently returning the precious packet to its proper place. *"Nonno* wouldn't come with us, but this . . ." He pulled his wife into his arms. "This will be the next best thing since his spirit will be infused in every plant that comes from these seeds."

As much as he wished they could linger, he suspected it wouldn't be long before Aldo appeared in his ancient, rattletrap truck. Fitting, considering the farmer was both the first person Rom had met when he'd returned to Santa Lucia, and the last he'd see when he departed.

By the time they'd cleaned the cottage, Aldo had arrived, leaning on his horn to alert the newlyweds to his presence. The flatbed of his truck was once again piled high with vegetables, though he'd saved space for them between the tumble of baskets, sacks, and wooden crates. "Or we can all squeeze into the cab," he offered.

"We'll be fine in the back, Aldo. Thank you for helping us."

After safely stowing the precious chest of seeds, he and Julietta climbed over the metal railings and made themselves comfortable on a pair of burlap sacks in the back. Before they departed, the photographer from the day before came running up, breathless.

"For you." He waved a packet in the air. "Your wedding photograph."

They took a moment to admire the candid shot before carefully tucking it away in the chest of seeds. Once they were settled, Aldo put the truck in gear, bucking and swaying along the narrow lane. A short time later, they reached the turnoff leading to Florence. Julietta's veil still hung in a waterfall of tulle from the signpost and they laughed at the sight. Slowly, the truck made the turn, grinding through its gears and gradually picking up speed.

Behind them, the past flowed off into the distance, half-hidden beneath a trail of dust. Rom—*Primo* now—gathered his wife close and deliberately put their backs to Santa Lucia. Ahead of them stretched endless possibilities. An entire lifetime of marvels to come.

Soon they would travel to a new land. Once there, they'd take *Nonno's* seeds and transplant all that was best from their former existence so it would become part of the new life they'd create for themselves. Like the plants, he and Julietta would have room to stretch and grow. Roots would spring from the seeds collected from their past and become the bounty for their future. As would their children and their children's children's children.

"I'd like a home on a hillside, Primo," Julietta said.

He nodded in agreement. "Overlooking the sea."

And there they would start a new generation of Dantes.

La famiglia.

One family.

Endless possibilities.

Yet, all borne from the life-giving flames of The Inferno.

The Dante Inferno continues with Lucia's story!

Forever Dante: Lucia by Day Leclaire

Meet Day Leclaire

I love family first and foremost, which is why writing a family saga is so much fun. Maybe you can tell that from my books since they always feature the warmth and joy that comes from having a close-knit family. I also love animals and have taken in rescue dogs and cats and fostered dogs for the local animal shelter. And of course, I love writing. All I need is a functioning brain (batteries not included), a pen, and paper, and I can write anywhere. Please don't let a conversation with me lag because my imagination takes over and I. Am. Checked. Out!

USA Today bestselling author, Day Leclaire is the author of more than 60 novels and has received an impressive eleven nominations for the romance industry's most prestigious award, Romance Writers of America RITA© Award. Day lives in Charlotte, NC and spends her days obsessively writing while vaguely remembering to pay attention to her adorable husband, busy son and daughter-in-law, two tiny grandchildren, and two even tinier Teddy Bear dogs. Not to mention a whole lot of dust!

Thank you so much for taking the time to read **The Dante Inferno:** *The Dante Dynasty Series*. I hope you enjoy this very special Italian-American family. I love hearing from my readers. For a personal response, please contact me at Day@DayLeclaire.com. And be sure to visit my website at www.DayLeclaire.com. Sign up for my newsletter for my latest releases and insider info available nowhere else! Just visit: https://www.dayleclaire.com/join-my-mailing-list

You can also find me on Facebook at www.facebook.com/Day.Leclaire.Private and Twitter at www.Twitter.com/DayLeclaire.